To Elizabeth

Enjoy

Where the River Bends

Christy Kyser Truitt

PRESS

I dedicate this book to the journey—the journey to live, the journey to dream and the journey to live your dream. And to the Shepherd who guides us down the right paths if we will only follow.

Acknowledgements

The first acknowledgement of any of my work is to my Lord and Savior. He has been so gracious to provide the words to this book and the time to write them down. I also want to thank my family for their patience, as always. Brittany, Abby, Billy and Trent know when mom is at the counter and the "click, click" is steady at it like tap shoes, to cut the TV down and to hear, "Yes, you do have to wait 'till I'm done." Thanks to my husband Brian for listening to my samples although I know he'd rather be gnawed on by fire ants than to read a love story. Your love and support is everything to me. Many, many thanks to Tim H. Martin, a talented wildlife writer and hunter extraordinaire. I appreciate your help with my hunting scene and wildlife noises. Thank you, Frannie, for all my "isms." And finally to the best friend a gal can have – my mom.

Prelude

*T*he dream was always the same, familiarity the only thing saving it from a nightmare.

Haven stood on the dock of her childhood home, arms outstretched in an attempt to protect the river from the destruction going on around her. Crowds gathered around her shore as she flowed along innocently, unaware of the activity on the outskirts of her borders. They yelled in expectation, history proving that bloodthirsty throngs inevitably gathered to watch death occur. Suddenly, the river shook, with a sonic boom sounding off the explosion. Haven never knew what was blown up, only that it destroyed the one connection to her past and showered her in the ashes of her youth.

CHAPTER 1

It's hard to find Jesus in a room full of sick kids, even if you're lucky enough to know where to look.

The room was oddly quiet. Should have been deafening given the ages of the kids that occupied it. But a steady humming and the occasional "Got him!" from the handful of leather recliners were the only interruptions. Movement came from the four silent televisions hanging around the walls as the kids wore headphones while playing video games or watching movies. Jimmy, the oldest at eleven, was steady, watching a slapstick comedy, mouthing the words from memory, while Sam KO'd some guy in Ultimate Fighting Championship: Throwdown on a PlayStation 3 a few feet from him. Madison was five and vigorously brushing her doll's hair, her lap filled with different color bows and ribbons. She wore headphones while a cartoon played on the TV in front of her recliner.

There were a few adults sitting stiffly beside the children, reading outdated magazines or staring out the window. Their faces were worn and tired and more than a little bored, if the truth were known. They only knew each other as Sam's mom or Madison's dad because you never knew who would be there on a given day. Disease was the ultimate equalizer, and you bonded over your child's condition whether rich or poor, black or white. It created an intimate relationship without being personal.

The April sun cruelly teased the kids to come outside to play tag or kickball or whatever it was that healthy kids did on a nice day. But the only sun these kids would see today would be setting. Freedom was years away in whatever form it chose to take.

These kids were sick.

All were on dialysis for various reasons—lupus, cancer, kidney disease. All were robbed of a childhood of innocence and recesses. All were trying to escape the disease of the day through the silent make-believe on the TV sets.

Jesus might have been there, but He sure was being quiet.

It was that same silence along with the white noise that had conned Haven into sleep, taking her away from the appraisal on a house she had spread across her lap. She was utilizing the downtime to calculate a fair market value for a new listing she picked up the day before. She needed to get some estimates to her customers so she could post the listing in the MLS this week. They were a military family, a relocation scenario all too familiar in their eighteen-year marriage, the wife had bemoaned. Haven came on the afternoon they called. They had a month before he reported to post, and while they needed to sell the house quickly, they couldn't afford to give it away. Somewhere in the back of the house, a door had slammed. "Teenagers," the wife had admitted sheepishly.

The work on the appraisal also gave Haven a brief respite from the demands of the pretty little girl fidgeting in the recliner next to her.

The white noise humming along was a dialysis machine, the pretty little girl her three-year-old daughter. Lauren was tied up weekly to a tube that exported the blood from her left arm, replacing the vital functions her genetically defective kidneys could not and then pumping the red life back into her tiny body through a second tube.

The fidgeting caused the appraisal report to slide off Haven's lap and scatter on the tiled floor. Haven jumped from the boundaries of her sleep, automatically reaching for her daughter.

"What's wrong, Lauren?" she asked. When she saw the familiar scowl clouding up Lauren's face, she fought to control her annoyance as she leaned down to gather her papers. It wasn't Lauren's fault. Wasn't her fault either. Wasn't anyone's fault. But it sure would be nice to blame someone else instead of always carrying the guilt herself. She caught the eye of a mother across the room who smiled as if relating. If they could talk, it might have gone like this:

"You know, it's okay to get mad," Sam's mom would have assured Haven. They'd shared a cup of coffee in the hall on more than one occasion, but little conversation. Haven knew she was married by the ring on her finger, but had never seen her husband. They told her that her son would die if the antibiotics didn't start to work on his infection. She'd be a pretty woman if not for the black circles under her eyes.

"Yeah, but who do I get mad at? Lauren? Myself?"

"All of the above. It's an honest emotion. Problem is, we can't show it. 'Cause showing it only makes it more real. Makes you show fear. And that's something, as mothers, we're just not allowed to do." But they never had that type of conversation. Never had the time.

Lauren interrupted her thoughts. "Don't wanna watch," she said, taking off her headphones while minding the constraints of her arm.

Haven knew without looking at the clock they were hours away from going home. She unfolded her long legs from a curled position and leaned forward to gather her papers. Sighing, she placed the stack on the table to her right and grabbed the available DVDs.

"I'm sorry, baby. We gotta watch about two more movies before we can go home," Haven said, using the time terminology suggested by the hospital's staff psychologist. "Here, let's pick out a new one."

She spread the movies in Lauren's lap and helped her decide between *Chicken Little* and *Shrek 2*. Unfortunately, Lauren had seen all the movies available for rent in her age group during the last year of dialysis. But having an active mind constantly fueled by an overactive imagination, it was difficult to keep her occupied and still. Early on, Lauren became so used to her treatments that she often napped through the greater part. The last few months, however, were tricky, as her naps and attention span became shorter and shorter.

Gathering her patience, Haven adjusted the low ponytail that captured her thick, wavy hair. A good romance book would describe it as "gathering the colors of dawn on the desert sand, spreading golden rays to permeate the blanched, sun-kissed earth."

Haven called it blonde.

When up in the tight bun she usually wore at the bottom of her neck, it was difficult to appreciate its unusual color. Really, there were few that ever saw it down. She always kept her hair long, but sighed her way through a cut to shoulder-length last year. It was just easier to keep up with.

Over the years, she learned to ignore the hard stares and suggestive looks from her male clients. A bathroom mirror to Haven was a means to check her teeth. It was the kind of beauty other women envied because she was able to take it for granted. She was approachable enough that women wanted to be her, and yet men, well, men just wanted her. It worked to her advantage as a real estate agent.

But none of it warmed her bed since leaving Sugar Bend. She knew she had to go, could never stay under those circumstances. Days after high school graduation, barely eighteen, she headed toward the Georgia coast in her white Toyota Camry, having never even crossed the city limits before except in her imagination. She remembered fear pounding her blood through her heart. But the freedom of being in control beat in cadence with that fear so she kept going. The first stop was for gas in the growing Georgia coastal town of Sweetgrass. Haven relied on fate to create this destination for her. She never once glanced in her rearview mirror. She eased off the accelerator only for approaching red lights and puppy dogs. It would take Lauren's illness years later to shatter that allusion of control, for that's all it really is, she would later discover.

She didn't realize her life was missing an element of purpose until the doctor placed a bundle of raw, screaming energy into her arms three years ago. This baby that seemed determined to announce her presence at an ear-piercing volume provided her mother with a sense of security she never felt before. It was the first commitment to another human being for both of them. And the world was suddenly a bigger, scarier place.

She ignored her whining child for a moment to breathe in the sight of her. Lauren was leaning back in the recliner, her bird-like limbs peaking out from underneath the blanket. She was so tiny that one often could mistake her for fragile, her weight no more than a large cantaloupe. Her black hair hung loosely past her shoulders onto her favorite pillow she brought from home, slightly ruffled from scooting all over the recliner in frustration. She was almost losing the white bow she insisted on wearing that morning. Her skin was a more normal texture now that the last year of dialysis had relieved its puffiness. Like her mom, she had a dimple in her left cheek, which remained indented whether she was smiling or not. It didn't look to Haven like there'd be much of that today. Lauren shifted in the chair, balling up like she was back in the womb, mad at a world that kept tying her down when all she wanted to do was run out in it.

The opening of the door to the dialysis room interrupted Haven's observation. Dr. Larry Jones walked in. She unconsciously fussed with the few strands of wandering hair that had fallen in front of her ears.

Dr. Jones had been a part of their lives since Lauren was diagnosed with polycystic kidney disease (PKD) last year. Her first meeting with the doctor occurred when she barged into his office carrying a very bloated and lethargic two-year-old in her arms. Haven had spent the good part of several days pouring over Internet sites, Googling Lauren's symptoms. Without knowing how she knew, she was convinced Lauren's problems were far greater than some bladder infection. After finding match after match for the symptoms to kidney diseases, she found the nearest doctor who specialized in her cyberspace diagnosis. She called for an appointment and was told to come in two weeks.

Not good enough. Her baby was sick. She was in his office the next day.

Dr. Jones recognized end-stage renal disease immediately. A later calculation of her glomerular filtration rate confirmed his initial diagnosis. Her renal function had dropped to less than 10 percent. She was retaining fluids, and her blood was poisoned.

Lauren was dying.

PKD is a condition in which many fluid-filled cysts developed in both of her kidneys and multiplied so quickly that it caused acute renal failure. There had been no symptoms, only the occasional urinary tract infection that Lauren's pediatrician had treated with antibiotics. But Lauren's kidneys took on the look of polka dots in the x-rays to the point that removal of the cysts was not an option. Her kidneys had ceased to function.

Dr. Jones, one of the leading pediatric nephrologists in the country, was on staff at Memorial Hospital in nearby Alabaster, only a ten-minute drive from Sweetgrass. While a teaching hospital, Memorial was renowned for its state-of-the-art hemodialysis center as well as therapeutic advances in the holistic approach to the treatment of pediatric kidney disease. Memorial insisted that emotional intelligence was just as important as physical healing. Children didn't have to stop being children just because they were sick. In fact, it was unusual for a dialysis center to be on site of a major hospital at all. It was more common to outsource this type of treatment to clinics where the doctor gives the patient a pat on the back, wishes them well, and sees them every six months at checkups. Not at Memorial. The hallways were painted bright pink and green; palm trees generously lined the halls and waiting rooms. The dialysis center itself was equipped with individual televisions with DVD and video game centers for each chair. There was always entertainment in the halls, from magicians to clowns to balloon artists. And while there was never any underestimation of why each child was there, it made the trip a little more bearable. At least that's what Haven read on their website and found to be true on her first visit.

It was unusual for Haven to notice that Dr. Jones was a shade under too tall, with dark hair peppered with gray. He had soft brown eyes that seemed to diagnose her internal thoughts just by glancing in her direction. She gave others' physical appearance about as much importance as she did her own—particularly a man's. There was no room in her life for romance; everything ebbed and flowed to her satisfaction. She answered to no one other than the needs of her daughter. But Dr. Jones had touched her with his attention to Lauren's moods and how he consistently treated her opinion as important. She guessed his age about forty, a little older than the few men she had dated. He wore his hair short and his sleeves long. And to the best of her knowledge, he was unmarried.

Dr. Jones noticed the scared yet expectant look each parent wore as he entered the room. He was used to it. They knew that at any moment, he could come in with life-altering news—sometimes good, but mostly not.

"How's my favorite patient?" Dr. Jones asked quietly after acknowledging all the other patients by name. The three moms and one dad returned to their routine of killing time without ever making direct eye contact with the doctor, relieved when he stopped at Lauren's station. He gave Haven a wink while squeezing Lauren's pink-polished toes that peeked out of the ends of her black sandals.

Lauren didn't answer, just crossed her arms over her chest with a scowl and turned her face into the recliner. She wore a yellow polka dotted dress with a lacy white collar, making her skin appear even darker than normal.

"Hmm. Looks like we're not having one of our best days. Let's see. How about I go see if Miss Janice has some gum? If she does, do you want me to ask her to bring it to you?"

"Yeah. Sure!" Lauren replied with more enthusiasm than she had shown all day, sitting up straighter in the chair, while mindful of the constraints of her left arm.

"You bet. I tell you what. Let mommy and me walk down the hall a minute and see if we can find Miss Janice. Here, draw me a picture in this coloring book until we get back," he said, pulling a book from inside his white, formal lab coat. A stethoscope hung around his neck, and a royal blue starched shirt peeked beneath his coat. He was neatly dressed, as usual, and Haven felt drab in comparison. She often dressed for work if she had an appointment scheduled around Lauren's treatments; otherwise, she dressed as she had today, in a loose-fitting sweat suit and tennis shoes. She dropped the footrest of her recliner and pushed up.

"YEAH!" Lauren exclaimed, her mood changing instantly as typical in three-year-olds and family dogs.

Haven squared her shoulders and strode purposefully through the door held open by Dr. Jones' right hand. She couldn't help but notice that the folder in his hand was Lauren's procedure file, and her stomach tightened. The two waited just outside the door until they saw Janice turn the corner toward the dialysis room.

Dr. Jones quickly took in his fill of Haven as she unconsciously brushed against him when leaving the room. For the past year, he had satisfied his thoughts of her with innocent brushings such as this and more pointed stares when she wasn't looking. His divorce lasted much longer than he ever would have imagined, and he was too proper to consider involving someone else in his personal mess. But Evelyn was now happily living in her Tybee Island home with her boyfriend/trainer, Manuel. He was more than ready to move on. He was just unsure how to do it after more than fifteen years of marriage.

Work filled his life; his pastimes included reading scientific reports on nephrologistic R&D. With his wife gone, he was content to create a family within his practice and enjoyed the relationships with his patients. It didn't hurt that all of them were under the age of ten. Safe. Controllable.

Completely unlike his marriage.

"The solution to all the world's problems isn't always found in your diagnostic reports," Evelyn had screamed at him one night toward the end. They were on the back deck, each holding a glass of wine like a weapon. She was small and blonde and full of fury. "You can't cure us, Larry, by taking blood and reading some x-ray. Sometimes you might actually have to talk to me long enough to figure out what's wrong!" But by then, the futility of their efforts was obvious, and they pulled the plug on their cancerous marriage. Or rather, their attorneys battled it out in mediation while Larry worked and Evelyn went to the Bahamas.

Those words, however, rocketed through his ears, bouncing along the ear canal until resting somewhere in the left temporal lobe of his brain. He knew she was right about his inability to fix his marriage. There were no scientific reports or case studies related to their specific symptoms. He wouldn't buy into all the hypothetical analysis Evelyn's therapist kept dreaming up. So he simply concentrated on those he could fix with order and precision.

And the scientist in him couldn't help but be intrigued by the anomaly of Haven. Sure, she was beautiful—textbook gorgeous, even. But she was also very smart, well-versed in Lauren's care, and surprising him with her research. He had watched her grow bolder through the years at interrupting if she didn't understand something and was quick to ask for a nurse change if the current one had difficulty with Lauren's port. She was Joan Fontaine in *Rebecca*, young and innocent until the darker side of life interrupted her inexperienced world. He loved that movie—everything neatly tied up at the end even if they had to burn it down to do it.

He recognized her poise at a fundraiser dinner for the dialysis center. He'd joined the conversation she was having with a small group of politicians by the buffet table. He watched her carry her side of a literary discussion of Faulkner versus Twain. One senator asked her thoughts on the illegal immigration issue, and she intelligently defended her conservative politics. But she never voiced an opinion to the taste of a New Orleans muffuletta or acknowledged one councilman's take on the dank odor of Market Street after a Charleston rain. And she merely nodded when the wives addressed the bold colors Bill Blass introduced at last season's fashion week in New York City, even though she was wearing one of his latest designs.

He knew she was successful in her own right. It said so in the paper. She dressed expensively, and he should know considering Evelyn's outrageous monthly clothing allowance. And yet more times than not, he was more attracted to the Haven Stunham that wore no makeup and lounged around the dialysis center in rumpled sweat pants. He could envision taking off the sweat pants with one hand and . . .

"This is killing me," Dr. Jones swore under his breath and unconsciously ran his hand through his shortly cropped hair. Reluctantly, he dragged his attention back to the task at hand and followed her into the hall.

When the door shut behind him, Dr. Jones pulled out his radio and called his staff nurse, Janice Portman, asking her to grab some sugar-free gum and candy he kept in the top drawer of his desk. He placed the small radio back into the pocket of his black pleated pants, took Haven lightly by her left arm. He led her into an unlocked room across the hall as soon as Janice rounded the corner.

"Haven, let's step into this conference room. There are some developments in Lauren's condition that mandate a change of procedure. Here, sit down, please," he said, gesturing to a chair on his right.

The room was rectangular, with coffee-colored grass wallpaper, customary tiled ceilings, fluorescent lights and a slight yet ever-present smell of ammonia. The more dominant smell was vanilla, commonplace throughout the hospital as related to its homeopathic approach to treating the patient rather than the illness. The hospital believed in the healing powers of both traditional and nontraditional methods. Aromatherapy was commonplace, as were strategically placed wildflowers, whose colors provided different healing effects as shown from studies in early twentieth-century England. The lights were unnecessary, as the wall directly in front of them was a floor-to-ceiling window giving a stunning view of the harbor. The spring sun waved at the unlucky to join its rays casting over the occasional sailboat that dotted the horizon like bobbing buoys in the soft waves.

When the two were seated, he continued. "Lauren's kidneys are beginning to show signs of rejection to the dialysis. As you know, polycystic disease often can be treated by dialysis indefinitely, but in some cases, a transplant becomes necessary.

"Now, before you panic," he said, laying his right hand over hers and giving a squeeze as he had done so often in the past, "remember that you're more than likely a candidate to donate a kidney to Lauren. If it's a match, it is a relatively simple procedure that has a good chance of healing Lauren completely. The surgery has some risk, of course, and is not pain-free for you by any means. We can discuss the details later when we know whether you're a match, but I don't want us to wait too long." He continued holding her hand. He'd transitioned to this familiarity over the last few months due to the amount of time Lauren's case demanded of him.

At least he had convinced himself that was the reason.

Haven looked dumbly at him with no response. In fact, his voice sounded like an upset drawer of silverware, and she wanted to stuff the words back in so they didn't enter her brain. She just wanted him to stop talking, period, so she could find some air to breathe in a room that suddenly had none.

But he would not stop talking.

She had an overwhelming urge to rip the tongue from his mouth. An unrealistic and rather unappreciative gesture, she would acknowledge later, but she was so tired of people bringing her bad news. She longed for someone—anyone— to come up to her and say, "Guess what? We've been wrong all along. We actually got Lauren's diagnosis messed up with some show we watched on TV. Isn't that great?" And they could all go home to live happily ever after. Don't shoot the messenger came to mind, but she wasn't sorry. She retrieved her hand and dropped her head to the table, inhaling the pine scent from a recent dusting. She didn't respond because to say it out loud would make it true.

"Haven?"

"I'm okay," she answered, straightening with some difficulty as her watery limbs offered little support. She reached for her ponytail to bite the ends of her hair like she would do as a child. She could hear the gruff voice of her father admonish her to "buck up."

"Okay, I hear you. I'm listening. I just can't believe we're here. She's been doing so well. I don't understand what happened."

"If you'll remember, we said in the beginning we were more likely to end here than an indefinite time on dialysis. She's in the early stages of rejection, but her numbers are definitely heading in that direction."

"But what happens if I'm not a match? I don't have any family alive. My mother left when I was a baby, and my father died the year before Lauren was born. I don't have any brothers or sisters, and neither did my parents. What then?"

That was the most personal information Haven had ever disclosed. She was always so private, determined to handle everything alone. Even now, the muscles in her arms were contracted to the extent he was afraid she would pass out if she stood up.

"Haven, do you remember the first time we got together to discuss Lauren's care? Remember how we talked about the power of positive thinking, about never giving up?" Dr. Jones asked, continuing when Haven nodded. "I wouldn't let you panic then over her situation, and I'm not going to let you start now. We've come a long way to improve her quality of life, and we need to look at this as one more step in the process. Let's take this one step at a time. If in the unlikely event you're not a match, then we'll have to prioritize Lauren on the donor list and say a lot of prayers," he said. After twenty years dealing with mothers and their sick children, he had yet to become immune to the emotions this scene always invited. Experience taught him that a firm voice often prevented a hysterical scene. Not that there was much chance of that from Haven. They were two battle-weary soldiers with a trust born out of necessity rather than personal history.

"But that can take years. How much time do we have?" Haven asked, her voice raising several octaves as the earlier wave of panic now rose like bile into her throat.

"Realistically, a year, maybe a little less. I don't want to put off getting you tested. If you can, I'd like to take you now to get started. Can someone come be with Lauren?"

Haven found familiar territory. As a single parent, the last three years was a circus act. Between her work, Lauren's constant sickness, and the occasional life interruptions of skinned knees and stomach viruses, it was juggling how to get from point A to point B, and who was available if she had to get to point F in between.

"I'll call Brittany and see if she can come over. If not, I'm sure Lila can. Just give me a minute." Haven retrieved her BlackBerry from her purse and punched in the familiar number of her babysitter. She didn't want to have to call her boss, knowing her busy day. Having confirmed Brittany could come immediately; she returned her attention to the rest of the afternoon. She knew she was free of appointments because she had a briefcase full of work to do while Lauren received her treatment. It would be another late night in order to get it all done. If she were lucky, Lauren would go to bed early, and she could work on that cost analysis that wouldn't get done this afternoon. She couldn't worry about the grocery store today. She hoped there was still at least one can of chicken noodle soup. She thought she had enough milk to get them through the morning so . . .

Dr. Jones cleared his throat, getting Haven's attention. "You're not in this alone, Haven. Again, let's just take this one step at a time," he said. Haven looked into his dark eyes and found understanding. It would be so nice not to bear this burden alone, but sharing it was not something she knew anything about.

"Thanks, Dr. Jones," she said. "You've been such a source of strength for us. I'm not used to leaning on anyone, so I'm not very good at it. But I'm glad to know you're here for Lauren and me. Thank you," she replied, forcing a softer tone when all she wanted to do was run back to her bed and throw the covers over her head.

"I think it's about time you called me Larry. It's okay to lean on a friend every once in a while. Let me be that for you," he said sincerely. His tone then returned to physician mode as he straightened the papers in Lauren's folder. "I've never asked about Lauren's father because quite frankly, it wasn't any of my business. But you've got to create options for Lauren in the event you aren't a match. I know you mentioned in our early sessions that Lauren's father was still alive. Would he be an option for her at this point?" he asked, looking intense while the mood in the room changed.

Haven sat back in her chair and straightened her legs under the table. They were long like a swimmer's, but the tight muscles stretched out were those of a runner. As she inhaled, she reconciled her mind to the fact that Lauren's father was an option. Somehow she knew she'd see him again. She just persuaded herself through the years that he wasn't an option for either one of them. She whispered his familiar name in her heart—Jake—as familiar as her own skin. The name itself spread a warm mist through her body while creating shivers on her arms. She hadn't talked to Jake since the weekend Harry died—the weekend of Lauren's conception. But she knew in her heart it would be inevitable. And she would have to tell him about their baby.

CHAPTER 2

The day Haven lost her father, Jake Baker almost lost his thumb.

"This is gonna hurt," Jake said to himself as he stared at the gaping slash just below the knuckle of his left thumb, wondering why it wasn't hurting already. He shook his head trying to remember what could have caused the cut. A minute ago, he was pulling out his pocketknife to cut through the binding strip holding the stack of plywood together, and then . . .

He swore out loud, remembering the whistling sound as the binding broke free and sliced through his thumb like warm butter. The searing pain made him forget his annual promise to his mother to stop swearing.

"Hey, little brother. What'd ya do this time?" Brad Baker asked, laughing as he rounded the corner of the framed house that their company was building. Brad was three years older than Jake, but the two were often mistaken for twins. Both were about six feet with broad shoulders forged strong from years of working construction and subsequently starting *The Baker Boys Development* two years previously. Brad was lean in his height, while Jake had the more athletic build. But both had the black hair and olive skin testifying to the Native American heritage on their father's side. Brad was turning thirty-one this weekend, much to his chagrin and Jake's amusement.

Jake lifted his gaze from his bleeding thumb and brushed the sweaty hair from his eyes with his good hand. *Great*, he thought to himself. *Here we go.*

"Well, big brother. This is called a work injury. Something you know nothing about because one would actually have to work in order to obtain it. While you are sitting around on your decrepit old butt, others are out here trying to earn a living so you can pay for your surprise party this weekend that you aren't supposed to know anything about."

Brad grinned at Jake, but that look quickly turned to alarm. "If you tell Beth I found out about that party, I'll have to break your other thumb. It was an accident I found out, I swear," he cried, throwing up both his hands in defense, tripping over the sawhorse behind him as he backed up.

"Yeah, I'm sure it was quite a coincidence that you were in Mr. Thomas' bakery acting like Beth sent you to make sure the cake was vanilla instead of chocolate. I would never accuse you of taking advantage of a seventy-year-old man who's half deaf, even if you did hit on his granddaughter in high school," Jake said, holding his good hand up to ward off any protestations from Brad.

"I did not hit on her. I went in there innocently trying to buy some freshly baked bread for our dear widowed mother when sweet Melissa asked me to help her fix something in the stove. She was all over me, not the other way around. Why am I always the one to blame? Can I help it if the women throw themselves at me? Man, I haven't thought of that in quite some time," Brad replied, his words dwindling as he lost himself in the memory with a sly smile on his face.

"Yeah, I'm sure it's hard to keep up with all of your conquests, Romeo. But before we continue this walk down memory lane, I need to run over to the emergency room and get a few stitches. I think I see some bone." He frowned as he studied his thumb.

"Again? You big baby, you got more stitches than a baseball. You always were such a pansy. Never could take any pain, always running to mama crying, 'Oh, poor, pitiful me. Lookee, Mommy, your baby who can't do anything wrong cut his wittle bitty finger.' You go put on your big girl panties and run along to the doctor." Brad taunted, but continued to back up, creating a wide berth around his brother. Despite his boastings, he was actually the brother who couldn't stand the sight of blood. He had passed out from simple splinters. As soon as their mom's sewing needle pierced the upper layer of his skin, he was gone. And that was before it ever started bleeding.

Unfortunately for Brad, Jake remembered this and shook his thumb as he passed, pleased as a spray of blood landed on his brother's feet.

Brad and Jake were inseparable despite their age difference. Brad stayed home after high school and took classes at the trade school to learn carpentry and such. Jake was the one who busted it weekends and nights to get his engineering degree by commuting an hour each way to the state university. Both worked long days to get the business off the ground. Even Brad's three-year marriage to Elizabeth Parsons didn't put a damper on NFL Monday Night Football. But it was their fierce loyalty to their widowed mother that made many a heart swoon over the years.

Jake entered the hospital hoping that Thursday mornings weren't peak hour in the emergency room. The only other patron was a mother and her small child, who would throw up a total of six times while Jake waited. He counted. Not that he had anything better to do. And yet it was still two hours before he was ushered back through the swinging doors. He imagined a round face with smoke pouring out around him existing just beyond the doors, administering hearts, courage and stitches at his wizardry whim. A short, big-chested blonde came around the corner in a nursing uniform that pushed her breasts together like freshly blown-up balloons—the kind you try to pop with darts at the weekend carnivals that always appeared overnight in Wal-Mart parking lots. His first thought was why they didn't date longer when they went out last year.

Then she opened her mouth.

"Hey, Jake. What'd ya do this time?" Brigitte Solomon said in a husky voice reminiscent of an old movie siren and yet too rehearsed to be real. Like her chest, there wasn't much about Brigitte that wasn't designed with the next schmuck in mind that crossed her path with a decent look. She took great care to angle her chest just right as she leaned over Jake's lap to observe his thumb.

"Why does everybody ask that? Is it too much to ask for a little sympathy around here?" he groaned, but nevertheless appreciated the view.

"Well, let's see. This makes the third time this month you've been in here, the second time for stitches," she replied, flipping through his file while pulling the curtains around his stall. "I lost count what this makes for the year, and it's only April."

"Just get the doc in here to take a look at it. I think I've got some nerve damage," he whined, the pain starting to kick in pretty good.

"There's nothing wrong with your nerve, darling. I can attest to that myself. Hey, some friends and I are getting together Saturday at The Cellar. Why don't you join us for some drinks after Brad's party?"

Jake considered the invitation. "I just might have to do that. I guess Beth's invited the whole town to Brad's shindig. But you know I can only take so much of all that marriage stuff before I start getting nervous. That is, unless I die from loss of blood waiting on Doc Stephens to make time for me."

Her fingers were cool on his arm as she adjusted the blood pressure cup on his good arm.

"I wouldn't figure you to be one to avoid marriage, honey. You went steady long enough with that Frannie Thompson in high school. I just knew when you didn't go away to college that you'd settle on down with her and load her up with a pile of kids."

Jake shook his head emphatically. "No, siree, not me. That marriage business scares me to death. I like coming and going as I please. I see how short a leash Beth keeps on Brad. I'm making it just fine on my own. I'm thinking it'll take a baseball bat on the side of the head to get my attention. Man, where is Doc?"

"Well, looks like I and every other breathing female over the age of eighteen are gonna have to practice our swings," she said, winking. "As far as Doc, you're going to have to wait more than a little while. It's my understanding they brought in Mr. Stunham about an hour ago in cardiac arrest. Last I heard, they were prepping him for open-heart surgery.

"I wonder if anyone knows how to get in touch with Haven or even where she is. I swear I never could understand how that girl could just leave her daddy after he raised her by himself like he did. Course, nobody could understand her, anyway, the way she just stayed down there on that river and never made any friends. Just shows you can raise 'em right, but it don't guarantee they'll end up right," she said, letting the air out of the pressure cup in a whoosh and taking the stethoscope from her ears.

Haven Stunham. Wow, it must have been at least five years since he'd seen her. The last time was when she slammed the door to her car and sped off, leaving her daddy in the dry dust of red dirt and gravel.

Jake had learned bits and pieces in the few days before she left. Harry had hired Jake to repair the railing around his deck that was damaged when a tree fell on it during the last big storm that had roared across the river bordering both their homes. Jake held the hammer in mid-swing when he heard Haven's voice carry through the cracked window of the kitchen.

"Harry, there's no way I'm leaving," she said in that typical stubborn voice. Jake was five years older than Haven. He watched her grow up, all bare legs and arms running through the woods along the riverbank. He never saw her in anything but cutoff jeans and a T-shirt.

"We're all each other's got, Harry. Just who's gonna take care of you if I go? And just where's it that I'm supposed to go?" she asked in an offended tone, although knowing the exact answer to the question. Anywhere but here. She knew Sugar Bend held no future. Haven chose to be a loner throughout her childhood years, preferring the woods and river to be her buddies. She knew she was different because she didn't have a mama. And she knew she had to leave just like her mama left her. She just didn't want Harry to know she'd planned it all along.

"Haven, you're more stubborn than Gracie on a bad day," he said roughly, referring to his gray goose that guarded the homestead. "I don't need you to take care'a me. I don't care what ya do. You just ain't gonna do it here. I'll not watch ya waste yer life away like some river rat in Sugar Bend. Go on, girl. Go make something of yaself for once."

"What if I don't want to?" she asked, surprising herself by the question. It was common for Haven to push back when pushed on and lose the war in an effort to win the battle.

"I'm not asking, am I? I don't care how old ya are. I'll still take a switch to ya. I'll not have you sass me, girl. Get your stuff packed and get. Ya ever think I might have me a woman? Couldn't never bring one around with ya here. Anything wrong with that? Now go on, get."

Jake continued hammering as the back door slammed. Haven ran off the deck. Although she knew what he said was exactly what she wanted to hear, it still hurt to think of Harry on the river alone. She knew he didn't have any woman. She knew he was pushing her away for her benefit—not his. And by the time she made it to the wooden dock, a hundred yards from the house, she remembered they weren't alone.

She glanced back up to the house and watched Jake working on the porch. He was a common fixture around their place those days, always ready if Harry needed some help. Growing up, she hardly noticed his presence. It was expected. Plus five years older might as well have been a hundred to an elementary and high school girl.

As Jake lifted the hammer, she noticed for the first time the muscles flexed beneath his white T-shirt. Her heart gave an unfamiliar jump as he stretched a long, blue-jean leg to hold one end of the plywood in place while he nailed the other end. His work boots were threadbare and muddy. Haven's breath caught when he lifted his shirt to wipe the sweat from his forehead. When he let his shirt fall, their eyes met and held for a moment, neither conceding to the other by pulling away. It was the roar of a passing ski boat that distracted both of their attention, allowing a silent draw between whatever forces just flew between them. *Wow*, she thought. Jake tried not to think at all.

It was three days later that Haven packed up her car and left, returning only for a few overnight visits. But Haven never knew that Harry would spend many mornings sitting on a bench down by the lake. But Jake saw it. He would fish most mornings in his honey hole just beyond the Stunhams' place. Without fail, a solitary figure would hunch over his Bible, occasionally lifting his face to the sky, eyes closed. The only light in the predawn hours would be the glow from a cigarette Harry would dangle from his mouth as he waited for the sun to tell him it was time to go to work.

Jake began going by the house after that, doing chores without being asked, occasionally mowing the grass. Harry would acknowledge his presence with a "humph" and then carry on with whatever he was doing. Through snatches of conversation, Jake realized that Harry had given Haven the greatest gift a parent could—the freedom to find her place. He knew from his outside view that Haven held a fierce loyalty for her father, and with just one request, she would have stayed here the rest of her life. He also knew that Harry suffered for letting her go. He would think back to a younger Harry carrying Haven around on his shoulders or standing side by side on the riverbanks casting a line. He must have realized it would have been selfish to keep her here. They both had to figure out life in this next stage for themselves.

While filling the push mower with gasoline about a year after Haven left, Jake stopped as Harry pulled up in his old Chevrolet pickup. He suddenly struck Jake as old, walking the crooked walk of someone that life had weighted down. He was all angles; his bones protruding through his leathery skin. When Harry gave his usual grunt that served as a greeting, Jake said, "Harry, I just want you to know that I respect what you did for Haven. For what it's worth, she never would've left if you hadn't cut her off like that. Well, I just wanted you to know that, for what it's worth." He bent again to the mower.

Harry stopped mid-stride and turned around with a look of raw pain, stripped bare from the usual gruff exterior. "Do something fer me, Jake. If something should ever happen to me, make sure Haven knows that. Make sure she's all right. She can take care of herself, that's fer sure. I don't know if she knows how to make herself happy. I didn't do a good job of teachin' her about feelings and stuff—figured that's all woman stuff. I ain't sure she knows about joy. Make sure she has joy. Do that, boy, ya hear?"

Jake was left alone with his thoughts while he waited for Doc Stephens. He sent up a silent prayer for Harry as his thumb throbbed and swelled beneath the fresh gauze Brigitte applied before leaving. He knew the joy Harry was referring to. He had asked his mama about it at a very young age after hearing the acronym J.O.Y. in Vacation Bible School. Mrs. Nelson had said it meant Jesus, Others, You, but that just seemed too easy for Jake.

"Mama, what's joy?"

Marianne Baker stopped wiping a pan for a minute and thought before answering. "Baby, joy is what you find when helping other people."

"Is that why you're always making cakes and stuff?" he asked, wiping his runny nose with the hem of his shirt. His mama rewarded him with a swipe of her dishtowel and handed him a box of tissues.

"Yeah, baby, I guess it is. I get my joy by making people feel better that are sad. I've got me a cake to finish up so we can run it over to little Joshua up the road. I heard his new puppy dog got run over this morning."

"Where's my joy, Mama?"

"Baby, you got to find that for yourself. Mama can't tell you where to find your own joy. It's personal. But you keep looking out for other people like you do, and you'll find it."

He hadn't had much opportunity over the last few years to visit Harry. Not since he and Brad started their own business. *No time for regrets now*, he thought. He wondered if he had time to call in some "PRs," as he and Brad called his mom's church group. They knew she was always putting their names on any prayer request list she could. Jake accused her on more than one occasion of using it more as an excuse to gossip by bathing it in a light of evangelical concern. Now that Brad was married, most of the requests were related to Jake releasing control of his life to the Lord and finding himself a good Christian woman.

He didn't realize he was left alone with his thoughts until the curtain to his area pulled apart, and Doc Stephens strode through. His face was lined with stress, his hair brushed over in a haphazard fashion.

"What'd you do this time, Jake?" Doc asked with no humor to his voice or face.

"Hey, Doc. How's Harry?"

Dr. Stephens closed the chart he was holding and pushed his glasses on top of his head. "We lost him, Jake. We were getting him prepped for surgery, and he just couldn't hold out any longer. Fool never would give up those cigarettes," he muttered.

Jake ran his good hand through his hair, suddenly sick of the smell of ammonia. "I hate to hear that. Harry was a good man. What about Haven? Does anyone know how to get in touch with her?"

"We haven't really gotten that far. I guess I'll call the wife and see if she'll run over to Harry's house and try to find a phone number. Here, let me take a look at that thumb," he said, unwrapping the bandages.

"Hey, Doc. You know I live a couple of miles up the road from Harry. I have a feeling I'm done with work for the day anyway with this thumb. I'll be glad to run over to take a look around. Harry gave me an extra key when I was doing some rot repair in his bathroom, but you know he never locked the door anyway. What does she need to know?"

Once the details were given, Dr. Stephens turned his full attention to Jake's thumb. "You're one lucky fella, Jake. I don't know how you can injure yourself as much as you do and not end up with something broken or damaged worse than it ever is. But you missed the nerve and stopped just shy of the bone. So it looks like all you'll need is some stitching up, as usual. I swear, boy, you ought to just invest in a good needle and thread and save us all some time. I'll send Brigitte in to do the dirty work," he grumbled, walking toward the door.

"Yeah, but it gives you purpose, Doc. I'm good for business," Jake called after him.

While the stitching hurt as bad as that time he had to work a fish hook out of his leg by pushing it through the skin, at least he was able to look down Brigitte's shirt while she sewed up his thumb. As he walked out of the emergency room door some three hours after he got there, the late afternoon sun caused him to squint as he heard the familiar chirp of his cell phone before he got to the truck door.

"Did anything get done while I was gone?" he asked without saying hello. He knew his brother, with all his false bravado, couldn't stand to see his little brother get hurt.

"Hey, pansy. How's the wing?" Brad asked.

"Well, eight stitches under the skin and eight stitches above, but no nerve damage. I'll be back to work next week."

"I knew you'd find some way to take some time off work. We somehow managed to finish up the framing while you were gone, but it did require me to break a sweat. The electrician is supposed to meet us on Monday morning, but I'll believe it when I see it. I'm going home now to take a shower 'cause I feel nasty. I think I broke a nail," he whined.

"File a Workers' Comp claim. You won't find much sympathy from me. Hey, bad news, big brother. They brought Harry Stunham in with a heart attack while I was waiting on Doc Stephens."

"Oh, man, that is bad. Is he gonna be all right?"

"Naw, he didn't make it. Apparently, they were prepping him for surgery when he had a big one that killed him. I told Doc I'd swing by his place and find out how to get in touch with Haven."

"Oh, yes, Haven. Haven of the legs that could wrap around you like a python and squeeze a man to death. She's got to be, what, early twenties by now? I wonder if she ever

37

found her figure?" Jake could picture Brad with his eyes closed, head leaned back against his car seat.

"Come on, Brad. Her father just died, and all you can think about are her legs and her figure?" Jake said, not admitting to Brad that was one of his first thoughts as well.

"You're right. Sorry. Good luck in that. I'm glad you're okay. I'll check on you tomorrow. I'm pulling in my driveway now, and Beth's leaning over the trunk. I can see that cute little heinie hanging outta her shorts," he said excitedly and hung up without saying good-bye.

Jake hung up laughing, reversed out of his parking space, and took a right onto Thompson Avenue through historic downtown Sugar Bend. The oak-lined drive took him past the only drugstore since the 1920s and old man Harding sweeping in front of the city hall. The town was small and flat; you could circumnavigate it on a bike without breaking a sweat. It always seemed dusty to Jake, even after a good rain – kind of like an old attic filled with things nobody would dare get rid of. It was one of the oldest settlements in Alabama, but too far west for Sherman's holocaust. Therefore, a majority of the homes were antebellum with historic markers planted like mailboxes. Originally called Awenasa, the Cherokee Indian name for My Home, it was changed to Sugar Bend after the Daughters of the Confederacy successfully lobbied for a more palatable moniker to promote post-World War II tourism. Jake drove straight through town, stopping at the four-way stop that joined the two competing banks, the post office, and the fire station, and over the river to the inter-weaving dirt roads that led to the houses below.

CHAPTER 3

The fifteen-year-old house was a two-story brick with updated appliances and an outdated roof. But Haven had already assessed its strongest advantage, a distant view of the Ogeechee River. So when she acquired the listing last month, she immediately received power of attorney and a budget from the deceased owner's children for home improvements. She hired tree surgeons to carve a natural window from the overgrown woods bordering the property. She then purchased two inexpensive wrought iron rockers from the local flea market, sanded them to a naked shine, and then glossed them over with crackled paint that provided the antique look so popular today. A few yards of outdoor fabric yielded brightly colored pillows. She borrowed plants from a local nursery to complete the look. Haven promised referrals in return. She glanced quickly at her watch, saw she had a few minutes to spare, and strode quickly to the master bathroom to freshen up before the open house began at one o'clock.

People rarely beat the door down at the beginning of an open house. But with homes in this price bracket; it was called a tour of homes for semantics purposes only. The afternoon would be a gamble. Sometimes you'd have a full house; often you just sat by yourself for hours. Haven took the time to check each room for the fifth meticulous time since she arrived some three hours ago. But she couldn't afford any mistakes. This was her first multimillion-dollar listing. It was THE ONE she had been waiting for since obtaining her real estate license three years ago. She found early success selling overpriced condominiums to parents eager for their college-bound children to avoid dormitory life. That had been her niche. But she knew even with repeat clients, she needed to break into the residential market. It was time to make her presence known.

This was the house to do it.

An hour into it, Haven was pleased with the response. Her instincts had been right about the atmosphere. While the house was certainly aged, with the right landscaping, it could be quite a showcase. She had created pamphlets on her home computer using a landscape design software program to show the potential of the lot, and it paid off. She already had one contract with contingencies and an appointment for a second showing the next afternoon.

"Oh my gosh. I just love it, love it, love it," the middle-aged brunette yelled at Haven, standing well within her personal space. Haven, uncomfortable with the close proximity, tried to back up unnoticed. "Edmund has just GOT to see this. I mean, would you look at this view?"

Haven knew that Edmund was Edmund Johnston of Johnston Enterprises Inc. He had stumbled across an idea using the same material in diapers for insulation or something like that and sold the patent for millions while retaining a paying position as chairman of the board. Regardless, the Johnstons could buy this house ten times over, and Haven didn't want to lose this client. She would just swallow with a smile the smell of the overpowering perfume stinging her nose with white lily. She merely arched an eyebrow at Mark, the other agent on duty that day, and was rewarded when he stifled a giggle behind his hand. Mark did giggle and giggled

often. He never had to come out of the closet about his homosexuality because he never entered one to begin with. Wives
loved him and husbands appreciated him because he safely
gave their wives the attention they never could be bothered
to give.

Haven was saved from a response when her cell phone
rang. It was Harry's phone number, so she excused herself
from the overly excited woman, touching her briefly on the
arm to compensate for backing away from her breath that
smelled of stale wine.

"Harry? Why're you callin' me so early?" Haven asked
cheerfully, her dialect returning to its origin of conjunctions
and ignored letters. "I wasn't expectin' to hear from you 'til
tonight." Although there were always excuses not to return
to Sugar Bend to visit, Haven regularly talked by phone to
her father.

"Haven?" a vaguely familiar voice sounded over the line.
Bad news immediately came to mind, and Haven quickly
walked into another room away from the crowd. She held up
five fingers to Mark giving an indication she could be a few
minutes. She closed the door behind her.

"Yes, who is this?"

"Haven, it's Jake. Jake Baker. You remember me?"

Remember him. As if she could forget the eyes that
held more than her attention so many years ago. While she
considered herself still a child at the time, it was very grown-
up feelings she took with her as she forged ahead with her
life.

"Jake. Of course I know who this is. Forgive me for not
recognizing your voice. Is everything all right?"

Haven's voice held an almost cool sophisticated quality
that unnerved Jake for a minute. It was hard to imagine her
grown up. He dropped down in the rickety recliner that he
assumed was Harry's port of call. It smelled of cigarettes
and coffee, but in an almost nostalgic and not unpleasant

way. He pulled his left hand through his hair and let out his breath.

"No, Haven. I'm afraid it's not. There's no easy way to say this, but Harry had a heart attack this afternoon. They were prepping him for emergency open-heart surgery when a blood clot entered his lungs and killed him. I'm sorry about this, Haven. I know how much you and Harry loved each other."

There was silence on the other end of the line, and Jake thought he lost connection until he heard a slight hiccup. "Haven? You okay?"

Haven sank down on the master bed and pressed her cell phone against her forehead. The bed was an enormous king-sized rice bed with a down comforter the size of summer clouds. The room itself was all white, providing Haven an almost ethereal environment as she slowly allowed Jake's words to penetrate her logical mind.

Harry was dead.

He was the only family she had. And now he'd left her, too. And while she'd always lived her life by herself, she was never alone. Harry was always a phone call or car ride away — if not for any purpose but grounding and familiarity.

"Haven?" A voice penetrated the thick fog that now engulfed her head.

"I'm sorry, Jake. I'm here. Where's Harry now? What do I need to do? Was he alone when it happened? How did he get to the hospital?" Her questions were flying out of her mouth like buck shots, but she was unable to control herself.

"Slow down, honey. Take a deep breath. I hated to have to hit you with this over the phone, but I couldn't find an address to come get you. All I found at the house was your phone number in a kitchen drawer."

It took a minute for his words to register. "You would have come here?" she asked incredulously.

Jake didn't pause before responding. "Sure, Haven. I know we haven't seen each other in a while, but I've been keeping up with Harry. He means a lot to me, or I guess meant a lot to me. No, he still means a lot to me. I guess what I'm trying to say is that folks shouldn't have to go through things like this alone. Do you wanna tell me where I can come get you?" Jake reached over the makeshift bar area to a mason jar holding several gnawed-on pencils with no erasers.

"Jake, you don't have to do that. Just tell me what I need to do, where I need to go. I guess I'll have to make all the arrangements. I can't even remember what Harry would want. Certainly no fuss, that's for sure." As Haven began to think of things logically, her pulse returned to normal, and a sense of control eased through her body. She could deal with this like any other business transaction. She'd make a working list, itemize the priorities, and get to work on the project of burying her father.

She'd just think of the reality of the task at hand later. Maybe next week when it all settled down. Until then, she had a job to do.

Haven found a piece of paper in the top drawer of the bedside table. She took meticulous notes as she cradled her cell phone between her right shoulder and ear, neat bullet points that she could check off once completed. She thanked Jake for his kindness and quickly pressed the off button, ignoring the thump of her heart when his strong voice said good-bye.

Jake sat back, and the recliner squealed in protest to his weight. He was puzzled by the resolve in Haven's voice. Maybe not puzzled, bothered would better describe it. She'd just learned her daddy had died, and yet he could hear the busy scratching of her pencil as she took down the information. There were no tears that were customary in all the girls Jake had ever known, tears that would come with the slightest suggestion of emotion, whether they were for the winner on a game show or the end of a really sappy movie. Jake remembered Haven as a little girl, never having girls over to play or lay out on the dock in her teenage years. Now that he thought about it, he never saw her date while she went to high school. Not that he remembered paying much attention, as he'd already graduated when she started ninth grade. He had long since lost his mind in the lean, cheerleader-muscled arms of his high school girlfriend. But looking back, he didn't remember ever seeing her with anyone other than Harry.

Maybe this is her way of dealing with it, Jake thought to himself. *But it can't be healthy.* Jake vowed to be there when Haven showed up at the funeral home to claim Harry's body. Whether she was used to company or not, he was gonna be there.

Haven walked to the master bathroom in order to check her appearance before rejoining the ever-growing house showing outside. For a minute, she just looked at herself, surprised at the face looking back at her. Outwardly, nothing seemed different. But she stared at her eyes. Why couldn't she cry? She had just lost her father, and yet all she could think of was step one, step two, and so on. What caused her to miss that emotional chip in her biological makeup? Why was there a sense of realized expectations as if she knew Harry would eventually leave her too? Her eyes certainly reflected strength, steely resolve, and an almost gritty determination. It was a rare time she admitted to herself that they held no warmth. No peace. No . . . joy. And yet she knew she was happy — at least by her own definition.

Haven thought back to Sugar Bend. She dreaded returning in such a public manner. Although Harry was low-key, she knew he was well-respected. He had the same job for the past forty years at the paper mill, always willing to work third shift so some of the younger men could be home to tuck their kids in bed. She also knew she would be expected to allow those same folks to pay that same respect to her father. Mentally, she began thinking of funerals in the South. Casseroles would be coming, and sweet tea pouring, only to where? She hadn't returned home in several months; springtime was always the busiest selling season for real estate. She had no idea as to the condition of Harry's home, so she immediately disregarded it as an option for some sort of reception.

Sugar Bend was still decades away from acknowledging a home on the river to be considered proper, much less desirable. In other parts of the country, however, the borders of all waters, both salt and fresh, were littered with million-dollar homes frequently visited by emptiness and only occasionally by their owners. But small-town South had a mind-set all its own that progress passed through on its way to a bigger destination. And everyone born there breathed a sigh of relief when it did.

She couldn't even think for a minute as to what type of service would be appropriate, for they'd never been particularly diligent about formal religious services. Maybe an occasional sunrise Easter service, but that was about it. Unless he failed to mention any spiritual rebirth, Haven would have to get creative. But she was capable of that. Haven tucked the endless questions behind the task at hand. It was easy to push her emotions behind the facade of business acumen that she had practiced so diligently through the years. She'd just grieve later, in private, like she handled everything else in her personal life.

The afternoon dragged on, but was successful by anyone's standards. While Harriet Johnston declined on signing a backup contract on this house, Haven had secured an appointment to show her several other properties she had listed next week. There was a particular two-story stunner secured by their agency just days ago that she knew would be the perfect fit. She knew the Johnstons owned several purebred Labrador retrievers, which Edmund used for duck hunting. Haven was already planning how to highlight the back yard, which could easily be redesigned to include a dog run and training area.

"Good work, Haven," Mark said as the two cleaned up leftover chicken salad sandwiches. "Looks like a great day."

"I think you're right. Certainly a lot more people than I expected. We'll just have to make sure Mrs. Johnston is taken care of." Haven wiped the counter before collecting her purse.

"Anything I can do to help you?"

"No, Mark. I appreciate your coming by. You didn't have to do that, but I'm sure glad you did. You go on now. I can finish up here."

It was late when she locked up, but Haven still had several hours of paperwork ahead of her. She was surprised at how her hand trembled when she opened the door to her car and folded her five-foot, eleven-inch frame into the front seat to start the ignition. *I need a good run*, she thought to herself, mistakenly placing the blame for her frayed nerves on a long day rather than allowing herself to think about the death of her father.

When she pulled into the parking lot of Coastal Real Estate Agency, she grabbed her gym bag out of the back seat. Not five minutes later, she was stretched over her straight legs in an attempt to loosen up her calves and hamstrings. Soon, she hit the pavement, running away from the setting sun, her iPod blasting hard rock tunes that no one would probably associate as her choice of music. Nirvana screamed at her to smell "teen spirit."

As she turned into Central Park, she turned the volume up a notch, increasing to a full-out run, her Nike shoes pounding the pavement in an attempt to run away from the emotions that were threatening to overcome her. How she loved to run. It demanded constant motion of her body while the hard rock music crowded her mind with the sounds of screaming men and electric guitars and nothing else. It allowed her for at least one hour a day to escape into a smaller world that was safe and consistent. Without warning, she stumbled, catching her fall with outstretched hands, but not before landing hard on one knee on the sidewalk. She glanced at the red blood threatening to spill over the scrape and remembered another type of bleeding from what seemed so long ago.

Haven wasn't older than eleven or twelve. Her body had yet to recognize its potential. Puberty was as elusive as a two-year-old at bedtime, dodging Haven as if she were playing hide-and-seek. Girls like Roxanne Williams and Pamela Lyons, along with every breathing teenage boy in their radius, were enjoying the ripening curves and filled-out chests that God had so graciously given this pretty set of girls who already seemed to have everything. Haven remained flat-chested, her unbelted jeans crumbling to her feet with no hips to catch their fall. It was this Haven that began the first day of sixth grade. Her hair was wildly loose down her back instead of the usual plaited pigtails in her clumsy attempt to join the ranks of the "I'm-not-yet-a-woman-but-I-darn-sure-want-to-be" club that the rest of the girls seemed to form over the summer. Unkempt hair was a sure sign of a mother-less household.

At least her housekeeper, Ruby, had enough foresight to hurriedly explain to her the mysteries of her menstrual cycle and to give her a mini-pad to carry around in her book bag.

"Ain't nothin' to be scared of, chile. Just part of bein' a woman. You can blame that woman Eve for havin' to worry about it at all's far as I'm concerned," Ruby told her when explaining the rites of passage. Haven wondered if Eve was some "trollop" that lived down by the bus station. Ruby would often whisper about that type of woman—whatever type that was—to her friends on the phone as Haven listened around the corner.

So, like every first day of school, Haven excused herself around all the mamas who walked their children to class, spitting into their palms to flatten the flyaway hair despite the protests. She moved silently, more of an apparition than a real person, and found her customary seat in the back. But her attempts at anonymity had the opposite effect. While her peers claimed individuality in their identical stonewashed jeans, teased hair, and off-the-shoulder Forenza sweaters, Haven stood in stark contrast with her simple T-shirt, naturally curly hair, and knee-length khaki skirt.

She tried to ignore her stomach as it continued its cramping and spewing that was typical of Haven's first day of anything she faced alone. Suddenly, a stronger cramp than usual tightened in her lower stomach. Haven waited for the increase in saliva that would signal the inverted march of her breakfast from her stomach. Instead, she felt a warm wetness flow into her panties and with horror, saw a rather thick and gooey, dark red liquid running down her bare leg and staining her white bobby socks she had so carefully folded down only hours before.

She knew without knowing how she knew that she'd just started her period. She waited for everyone to notice. She never felt the hand on her shoulder until it gave a gentle squeeze.

"Haven, honey? I'm Mrs. Delsam, your homeroom teacher. Honey, you okay? Oh my," Mrs. Delsam said as she looked over Haven's unmoved head and noticed the stain forming on the floor. She quickly moved around Haven, taking off her jacket and blocking the view from the rest of the classroom.

"Don't you worry about a thing, honey," Mrs. Delsam reassured her quietly. She knew about Haven's situation;

her husband worked with Haven's daddy at the paper mill, and she eagerly anticipated Haven's arrival. Haven thought she looked like the fairy godmother that came to rescue Cinderella. She remembered watching the movie in the library during summer break after third grade and wishing she had a grandmother just like that. Mrs. Delsam quickly wiped Haven's blood from the floor with one side of her gray fleece jacket that she bought on sale at Kmart. She somehow got Haven to her feet, wrapped the jacket around Haven's waist and walked with her to the door. Haven was numb with the anticipation of a roomful of laughing faces at her. She grabbed the ends of her hair and began biting while Mrs. Delsam told the rest of the class that she and Haven would return in just a minute. No one seemed to notice, as they were too busy arguing about who was going to sit by whom and discussing from which catalog each new outfit was bought.

Haven learned more from those five minutes in the bathroom with Mrs. Delsam than her entire well-intentioned and yet inadequate conversations with Ruby. Ruby was more set on quoting Old Testament Scripture than equipping Haven for crossing the elusive threshold of womanhood. Luckily, her bleeding was contained to the inside of her bare leg and the top of her sock, so only a whispered explanation was necessary to Harry when he picked her up from school. Haven's prayers were answered by a silent ride home. She bolted from the car and ran to her mirror to finally witness the culmination into the woman she was so anxious to become. Although her same image reflected back, Haven noticed for the first time an energy that radiated just below her translucent skin. It would ultimately shield her from the self-imposed isolation of her teenage years.

But it was the kindness of Mrs. Delsam that would later contradict her recollection of an entire town that would not accept her. She refused to allow such reminiscing to challenge the validity of her initial decision to leave. And it was these conflicting memories that would line the roads of Haven's return.

CHAPTER 4

Haven lost time on the sidewalk. She couldn't stop crying long enough to be embarrassed by the spectacle she was creating. She waved off several concerned passersby, worried about the beautiful woman crying over a scraped knee. But she couldn't stop. For the first time in her life, she allowed herself to actually feel the emotions associated with her lifetime of emptiness and wept.

What seemed like an eternity was really an hour later that Haven entered the backdoor of the real estate agency. The old brownstone tucked away in a side alley in the historic district had been a refuge for Haven since she first entered the office about four years ago. She had found a flyer at a hamburger joint just outside of town that advertised low-rental properties. After receiving directions from the hairy, tattooed owner, she found her way to Coastal Realty.

"You tell that sexy Lila that Hairy Larry told her to get those juices goin' 'cause I'll be over to get her later," he called after her, shaking a dirty spatula in the air.

Haven sat in the lobby discussing potential rental properties with the young college student whose nametag said "Abby" when the door opened. If life itself were personified, it would look like Lila Adams. She merely floated through the door on a cloud of diamonds and Chanel No. 5 perfume.

She wore a well-cut beige suit trimmed in fur, although it was bordering on hell's oven temperature-wise. But Lila looked as refreshed as if she generated her own air-conditioning system. She appeared tall to Haven, until she noticed her three-inch black patent leather stilettos that carried her trim ankles across the floor.

She smiled at the assistant who had introduced herself earlier. "Darlins, darlins, darlins, what have we here? Abby, who IS this stunner sitting at your desk? Do we have a job for THIS girl? She's a real estate agent if I'VE ever seen one. Darlin, I'M Lila Adams. I own this HERE little juke joint. And I'm telling YOU that YOU are going to quit whatever road YOU are on and jump in the car with ME to Successville!"

Haven didn't realize this was the first time in her life she had actually been introduced to someone. The first time you met someone in a small town you were still young enough to be best friends or natural enemies immediately. There were never any formal introductions.

She was immediately shy.

Lila had that beautiful southern accent that was indigenous to the true South. Not the exaggerated version any true southerner winced through in the movies. No sir. Miss Lila was southern to the core. She was a former Miss South Carolina, Kappa Delta president at the university where she proudly wore her blue jeans with her pearls. When excited, she spoke every other word as if it were in capital letters. And Haven would come to find the surrogate mother she had yearned for her entire life.

From that day forward, Lila took Haven under her wing. She would never understand why this incredibly successful woman took such an interest to her, but she was too smart not to recognize she owed her everything. In the next four years, Haven would complete her studies in real estate, become a licensed broker, steadily move from her original one-bedroom apartment over the garage of one of Lila's friends to a one-bedroom condominium several blocks off the historic district to the three-bedroom cottage she now lived in off the bay. She watched her bank account grow with each real estate sale, beginning with simple transactions involving rich college students whose daddies thought it was smarter to buy than rent and eventually to the fast track she was on today. If she could not only secure the Johnston deal to sell the property they already had listed, but also work a deal to list their home as well, it would mark the third multi-million-dollar property listing under her credits this year alone! It was unheard of in such a competitive industry. And she owed it all to Miss Lila.

Haven noticed Lila's office door was open as she crept down the hall, wiping her forehead with a white terrycloth towel. Just as she passed the door, she heard, "Haven? That you, honey? Come on in heeyah a second." Lila's r's sounded like ah's, so "here" became more like "heeyah." Her sentences truly drawled in an unhurried fashion that was typical of the South. It was just too hot to talk any faster, and the South tended to drop unimportant consonants like an embarrassing relative at a family reunion. Haven stopped for a few seconds to collect herself, rubbed her face with her towel in an attempt to mask the puffiness of her eyes, pivoted on one heel and entered the plush and immaculate office.

The wheels did not even squeak as the fifty-three-year-old turned in her navy blue, nail-trimmed chair to face the open doorway. Her black-framed, white polka dot reading glasses were perched atop the wildly coiffed naturally auburn hair. Taken in pieces, Lila Adams was not beautiful by magazine standards. Her mouth was a little large for her face, her eyes a little too far apart. Her lips were thin, and her hair always looked as if it lost squatter's rights to a squirrel. Furthermore, her body was not fashionably stick-thin, but rather curvaceous, buxom with tiny feet that looked like pedestals under a potted plant. But the total package was illuminating, lighted afire with a personality that announced Lila's presence before you ever saw her. She had the energy of women half her age and the sex appeal of an old Hollywood screen goddess. But it was her loyalty that drew Haven to join her company to replace Abby, the receptionist, who was graduating college. Once Lila confirmed the way people responded not only to Haven's beauty, but to her genuine goodness, she groomed, coached, needled, and fussed until Haven emerged into a professional, sophisticated woman whose potential was unlimited in the industry.

"Dahlin, come sit. I heard you put on quite tha show down on the bay today—do tell, do tell," she said, waving her hands in front of her as if fighting off the river gnats that the waters of Haven's childhood coughed up at sundown. "Wait a minute. What's wrong with you?" She held up a hand to ward off Haven's protestations before they even started.

"You've been cryin'. DON'T tell me you haven't and DON'T tell me nothin's wrong. You WILL tell me, or I'll rearrange your files out of alphabetical order and break the tips off ALL your pencils you sharpen every mornin'." Lila strode purposefully across the plush ivory carpet in her customary heels and shut the oak-paneled door. She returned to the empty chair beside Haven, turned in it to face her, and leaned to take both Haven's hands in hers.

"Spill it."

Tears immediately flooded Haven's eyes, threatening to spill as she turned them up, willing them to go away. As if on cue, they did.

While Lila studied her, she said, "I got a phone call earlier that Harry died. It was unexpected. Apparently, he had a heart attack while they were preparing him for surgery. I've got to take some time off to go to his house and make arrangements. It shouldn't take more than a few days. I'll get the appraisal ordered on the showing today, and maybe Mark can take Mrs. Johnston to lunch to help make up for my putting off my appointment." Haven trailed off as if forgetting what she was saying.

Lila looked at her with concern. "Oh, dahlin. I'm so sorry. I liked ol' Harry. It kinda hurt my feelings you never bothered to fix us up. Lord knows everybody else in this county has tried to do that. I don't want to hear another word about work. Let's figure out what we need to do. When do we need to go? I can clear my calendar today."

Haven genuinely laughed this time at the thought of this grandiose woman in her father's company. It would be like taking a barn cat out to eat with a Tennessee walking horse. And yet she was not surprised by Lila's offer. Lila would walk through fire for Haven. It didn't take long for her to trust that; it was almost instinctual. Lila was one of the very few people, the only one now that Harry was dead, that Haven truly trusted with her heart. And she was touched by the offer.

"No, Lila, that's not necessary. I won't be gone long. I'll make some calls before I leave, get it all arranged so that I won't have to stay long. Besides, who'd take care of Sir Gally?" Sir Gallahad was Lila's Yorkshire terrier and, as far as Lila was concerned, her only blood relative. After Lila survived two husbands, Sir Gallahad provided her with all the companionship she could ever want. Or so she said.

Lila got up and circled her desk, picking up the phone while saying, "Don't you worry about Sir Gally. He's an independent old cuss as much as he pretends not to be so's not to hurt my feelings. Let me call Joanne, and I'll book us a flight."

Before she could dial, Haven protested, "No, Lila. Honestly, this is something I need to do for myself. It's not that far a drive. But I do appreciate the offer," Haven said, standing somewhat stiffly as if a heavy weight was pressing on her shoulders to keep her down. "I'll be fine, I promise. I'll even call when I get there and let you know how things are going."

After several more minutes of reassurance, and a few pecks on the cheek, Haven slipped back out of the rear entrance and made her way to her townhouse to begin preparations. Lila returned to her desk, but not to her work. She turned her chair toward the open window, trying to decide how to best help Haven.

"What's your take on that?" An almost feminine voice asked from the doorway. Lila jumped around in her chair with surprise.

"Mark, you scared me to death. I swear I'm going to put thumbtacks on the bottom of your loafers so you'll quit sneaking up on people like that! What do you mean, my take?"

Mark walked stealthily into the room. He was as graceful as a cat, but as stocky as a linebacker. His fluid motions carried him through Alabaster's high society long before he graduated high school some fifteen years ago. Although openly gay since his teenage years, his mother merely whispered in polite company, "Mark's just a little more sensitive than most boys." And her friends in their pearls and pumps merely acknowledged her understatements with raised, finely plucked eyebrows, a nod, and an "ummm hmmmm." His retired military father just played golf.

Mark lowered himself into the chair previously occupied by Haven and said, "Come on, Lila. You don't have to protect Haven from me. Something is up big time with Miss Thang, and, as the only male in her life, I have a right to know what it is. Tell Uncle Mark how he can help."

Mark listened intently as Lila shared Haven's news and plans for the rest of the week. "I wish she would let us go with her, but she's as stubborn as that red wine stain on my carpet from last New Year's Eve. What do you suggest?"

Mark pondered for a moment, tapping his right index finger against his chin. "Well, I always use baking soda mixed with water and give it a good scrub. Oh, you mean Haven?" he joked as Lila frowned, then turned serious. "Give her space. Let her go home by herself. Do you even know how far back in the woods that is? She's never talked about it much to me. I get the feeling she grew up pretty much alone, so we may crowd her unnecessarily if we push," he said, staring off past the landscape paintings that adorned the back wall in appropriate groups of three. "I'll stop by her place tonight before church. She borrowed my Persian throw rug for a staging a few months ago. That'll be a good excuse to drop by. I'll put my big toe in and test the waters then."

"You always know where to put that toe, don't you? Now, what's this about church?" Lila never bored hearing of Mark's latest adventures and settled into her chair to catch up. Mark was a paradigm. He was deeply religious, although not committed to a particular denomination. But he found solace and structure in the words of his Bible that he never had in his childhood home. And still couldn't find in his personal life.

"I thought I'd visit that new nondenominational church out in the county. They're having a revival tonight. Figured I could compromise another fellowship with my homosexuality," he spoke with humor and an underlying tone of resignation.

Lila remembered Mark admitting several years ago that he was quietly asked to leave the church he grew up in—the church his mother still attended. She couldn't remember now the excuse that was given. It was obvious that it was due to his sexual orientation. But Mark's heart yearned for the rituals of the traditional church service of his youth, and she hoped this church would give him that. That was always her problem with these old churches. They seemed so exclusive rather than inclusive. Lila thought all the talk of hell, fire, and damnation was just tacky and a little too dramatic for her tastes.

She sighed. "When are you going to stop defining yourself by your sexuality?"

"Why should I? Everyone else seems to."

Lila frowned at him. "Honey, you know I can't quote the Bible like you can, and that young Mandy we just hired can run circles around me in a sanctuary. But I can't help believe that Jesus goes about things a different way than we might think. It's His job to convict you—not yours. I'd listen to Him a whole lot quicker than anyone else."

Mark seemed to ponder that a minute. Lila backed off.

"Guess that's my cue to shut up," Lila laughed, coming around the desk to grab Mark's arm before he left. She put her left hand against his cheek. "I love you, sweet boy. We've been through a lot together. Prune away some of those trees that block your forest, darlin', and take a glance at what's around you. You may find somethin' you like—maybe even yourself."

Mark smiled and placed his hand over hers, brought it to his lips, and kissed it tenderly.

CHAPTER 5

J ake spent the next day around the Stunham place, getting things pruned and cleaned up before Haven's arrival. Oddly, her image seemed to be everywhere, which surprised Jake. He didn't realize he had so many memories of Haven. As he struggled with a particularly stubborn vine wrapped around the box hedges anchoring the corner of the house, he remembered Haven sitting down at the dock with her feet dangling in the early winter water.

"You're going to freeze your butt off, Haven. What are you thinking?" He remembered yelling at her from his boat several hundred yards out.

"Don't worry about me, Jake Baker," she yelled back. "Ice runs through my veins!" She must have been about thirteen then, wearing a plain navy hooded sweatshirt and rolled-up blue jeans. Her hair was tossed wildly about her shoulders. Its paleness gave her the look of fairies Jake's mama used to read about in bedtime stories.

He wondered now if anyone ever read her stories. He didn't know that Haven read herself to sleep each night with poetry. Robert Frost and Walt Whitman lulled her to sleep with words about the woods and water. But the words that sounded in her head were not in her own voice. She read to herself in a soft, womanly voice in an accent she imagined to be northern, having never met anyone from outside Sugar Bend. A voice she imagined to be her mother's.

Jake pulled his boat up to the dock and deftly tied the rope to the anchor beside Haven. Uninvited, he sat down beside her, slipped off his shoes and socks, and carefully put one big toe in the water.

"Crikes!" he screamed, pulling it out as if escaping the mouth of a rattler. "You're crazy, girl!"

Haven started laughing. "What did you say? Crikes? Is that even a word?"

"Well, it is in the Baker house so my mama never hears me cussing. We had to make up words to take their place. Mine was 'crikes,'" he boasted proudly.

Jake could feel the knife of the freezing water even today, some nine years later. But more clear in his memory was sitting so close to Haven. Her skin held a constant blush of too much sun even in the winter. But it was her smell that Jake recalled most vividly this morning. She smelled like the woods. A light dusting of morning dew mixed with an earthy, fruity smell that didn't come from any bottle. It came from a childhood of nature mixed with a little . . . . Jake struggled to find the word.

Loneliness, he thought to himself. That's what he smelled the most in Haven. And yet she never seemed lonely, just always alone. Jake had forgotten all about that early morning time with Haven—the two not saying a word other than the occasional chuckle from Haven and an elbow to his ribs as she silently made fun of his inability to withstand the cold water. Every once in a while, she'd say, "Crikes" under her breath and giggle.

Shaking his head of the memory, Jake returned to the task at hand. What should have been easy was made more cumbersome because of his injured thumb. He noticed blood seeping through his bandage and winced at the thought of busting some stitches. Luckily, it was a surface scratch from a thorn on the vine, so he continued steadily working. He then felt a slight nip on his left ankle.

Whirling around, he was face to face with a growling goose, gray head bent low as if she were a bull facing the matador.

"Now, Gracie, what is your problem? You know me, cut it out," Jake said, shaking a fist full of vines at her. Harry had Gracie as long as he could remember. Other than a few chickens, Gracie was the only animal the Stunhams ever owned. Jake remembered bringing a puppy over for Haven when she was little, only to have the tearful eight-year-old return it the next day. Gracie had chased the poor thing up onto the porch, where it promptly peed on the welcome mat while scratching a hole in the screen door.

At the sound of her name, Gracie raised her head and looked around the yard. When she returned her gaze, Jake swore he saw sorrow reflected in her brown eyes rimmed with green.

"I know, girl. It's strange not having him around. Come on, let's go on over to the shed and see if we can find something to eat."

The Stunham place was originally some eighteen acres with one hundred feet of waterfront. Over the years, Harry had bought up surrounding lots, mostly because he feared any development that new bridge might bring. But he didn't have to worry about the Bakers' cabin, located just around the bend on a few acres of near-marshland. Bill Baker never would have sold his weekend fishing hole. Harry grew to trust that neither would his boys, now that Jake lived there full time.

The Stunham homestead was a rectangular plot with a pine shed topped with a tin roof just up from the water that held chicken feed, Harry's outdated push lawn mower, and a broken-down tractor he kept telling Jake he was going to fix. One day he was going to ready some of his additional acreage for corn. It looked as if a good wind would put it out of its misery, but it stayed strong. The shed was up on stilts, like an old lady that pulled up her skirts when stepping through a mud puddle, tilted slightly like she had a few too many. The house stood about a hundred yards off the water, lifted off the ground for the same purpose as the shed. No river house was ever built on a slab. Well, no one native to the occasional flooding ever did so, anyway. It was single-story, mostly vinyl siding with a deck that lay like an open palm against the house, inviting anyone to come in, as the door was never locked. Not many ever did. The only windows were the sliding door off the deck and smaller ones up to the right, which looked into the kitchen and Haven's childhood room. A long gravel driveway snaked around the side and up through the pines to meander back to the main road leading to the bridge.

Jake couldn't help but compare Harry's home to his own in town growing up. Luckily, William Bradley Baker held a sizeable life insurance policy. Combined with the insurance settlement from the drunk driver's estate, it paid off all the Bakers' debt and held a trust for the boys. Years later, it would subsidize their income while they began their construction business. It allowed Marianne Baker to work part time while her boys were at school and to be home when they returned, freshly baked cookies and milk at the table. The yard was small, allowing only a small grumble from the boys in springtime when it required a half-hour's worth of mowing. But Marianne had created a blooming wonderland with gardens of hydrangeas, hostas, lantana, and sprawling verbena in explosions of color and backdrops of green. And one native oak that could be seen from space anchored the yard as if guarding it from any more grief. She lost the love of her life after sixteen years of marriage, and rather than let her small boys see her grieve, she attacked the dirt in her home and garden as if it were guilty of the crime itself.

As a result, the house was constantly full of the laughter of young boys, the slamming of the door bringing in or spitting out dirty feet and smiling faces. Cookie crumbs trailed through the house and onto the front stoop as if leading straight to a fairy tale witch's door. And life went on with everyone trying to stay as busy as possible so that boredom would not give sorrow the opportunity to overwhelm the happy home.

Though economics segregated his town growing up as surely as the color of one's skin, athletics was the great equalizer among southern boys. Even if Jake couldn't afford the latest fashions or drive the coolest car, he could still crack one over the center fielder's head on a full count, which allowed him to appear at the top of every party list and graduation registration in town. Not that there were many.

As Jake carefully threw some feed in Gracie's direction, hoping to improve her disposition, he looked in the distance to the right, down the river and over a grove of trees anchoring a bend in the water. He could just make out the construction site of the new bridge. It was too long in coming. And like anything involving the government, it would take too long to complete. But like most everything in life, it took death to create change. *Death may be too dramatic a term*, he thought. *Maybe it was just the end of things.* The old bridge held many memories, both good and bad. There had never been a senior class at Sugar Bend High that didn't jump off that bridge, despite the warnings of possible incarceration. Billy Turner, the local law enforcement officer, always stayed at the end of the bridge, ready for an emergency, but never an arrest. He loved those kids and having jumped off the bridge himself some seventeen years ago could never bring himself to do anything other than pray for a bobbing head once it plummeted beneath the muddy waters.

But it was the fatal head-on collision of a state representative's son that finally got the state to approve the new $6.5

million, four-lane bridge that was set to be completed in the next few years. The state would then blow up the current two-lane rickety "Tinkertoy" that existed today. Jake for one wanted to be the one to push the button on the explosion, for it was that bridge that killed his father. Well, technically, it was the drunk, middle-aged veterinarian who was racing from his latest mistress' house, trying to beat his unsuspecting wife home from choir practice. But the bridge was the tombstone over his father's grave that Jake visited every morning on his way to town. He would be glad to put it to rest.

The sun was hot on Jake's bare shoulders. He had peeled off his sweaty shirt hours ago, and it was the tingling of a coming sunburn that reminded him of the time. He glanced at his cell phone, dangling from the clip on his belt, and realized he had only about forty-five minutes to meet Haven at the funeral home. It didn't occur to him that he might be intruding. He was raised that neighbors took care of each other, and that was that. His mother had spent most of yesterday cleaning out the house and stocking it with homemade monkey bread, fresh coffee, and assorted casseroles in the freezer. Sadly, it no longer smelled of cigarettes and old whiskey, which was the perfume of choice for Harry Stunham. Now, it boasted the pine-fresh smell of ammonia and sparkling linoleum floors, which took four scrubbings on hands and knees to remove the years of boot treads. The house was neat, not much in the way of scattered papers or spoiled food. Harry was tidy, if anything. But twelve-hour shifts at the paper mill didn't entice a man to hit his house with a duster and mop on a regular occasion.

Jake returned the rake to the shed and made his way to the dock. He unzipped his Levi's, pulled them down over his narrow hips, and let the sun wrap his boxer-clad body like swaddling a newborn. Finally, he shed his boxers and dove headfirst into the river and stayed under for as long as his lungs would allow. It reminded him of the game the Baker boys would play, to see who could hold his breath the longest. Jake grudgingly admitted that he never could beat Brad. *But then again, Brad really wasn't anything but hot air, anyway*, he consoled himself.

The water was a warm seventy degrees, but Jake found several cool spots that teased his toes. Unmindful of his nakedness, he lay on his back and breathed in the spring air that held the promises of a scorching summer. He thought of Haven again.

"You catching anything but time?" she had called to him from the dock. Her long fingers saluted the noonday sun, her left hand holding a book by her side. She was always reading something. She stood tall against the backdrop of her home. He could just make out Harry in the distance, struggling to get the push mower going.

"Wasting time is more like it. I don't think there's enough books in print for you, girl. What are you reading this time?"

"Steinbeck's *Of Mice and Men*. You might have heard of it, considering it's a classic. Then again, you probably know more about the movie than the book," she teased. "You're definitely a George, and maybe I'll be your Lennie."

"Ha ha, whatever that means. Why don't you put down that book and take a ride with me to keep me company?" he had asked, surprised at the thought. He was twenty at the time and dating Sally Jordan, the new teller at the bank who had just moved to town, after he'd broken off a three-year relationship with his high school sweetheart.

"Sure thing, George, pull on up," she answered. Haven was fifteen, but a slow bloomer. Brad used to needle Jake for spending so much time fishing around their house.

"What's your deal, bro? You robbing the cradle or some-thing? Man, she's just a kid," he would say, combing out his mullet in his meticulous fashion. The black comb was for the bathroom, a red one stayed in the console of his Trans Am, and a yellow one remained in his locker. He was voted Best Hair for three years running at the "Who's Who" banquet at school.

Haven placed her well-worn novel on the dock and easily stepped into the boat without leaning down or creating the slightest disturbance. She folded her long legs beneath her as she stepped over the built-in seat of the johnboat and settled into the bottom, her back to him. As Jake shoved off, she picked up a pole from beside her, grabbed a slimy earthworm with two fingers from the tin bucket, and easily slid it over the hook. Although owning a tackle box worth boasting about, Jake found a sense of origin fishing with the worms. He used his trolling motor to inch a few yards out and then cut the engine, leaving them in the company of the late afternoon river. The only sounds were the gentle lapping of the water against the bank and the distant rat-a-tat-tat of cars grinding their way over the antiquated two-lane bridge connecting the River Ones, as the landowners were called, and Sugar Bend.

"Can I ask you a personal question?" Jake inquired, breaking the silence. He had been looking at Haven for a few minutes, admiring the way her white shoulders were sprinkled with freckles under the hot pink spaghetti straps of her tank top. "How come you don't ever have any friends over?"

Haven was silent for a while; so long that Jake thought she wasn't going to answer. Without turning around, she said, "I guess I don't really have any friends, Jake. It's not that I don't like people, I guess I just like being by myself. Always have been, except for Harry. All the other girls from school just like different things. I'm not into cheerleading or beauty pageants or stuff like that. I don't know how to fit into those houses that have a mom, dad, brother, and apple pie. Not my style." She reeled in her line at the end of her response, reeling in the conversation as well. As she recast, she looked over her shoulder and gave Jake a slight smile, showing the dimple in her left cheek. "I guess you're the only friend I got."

As Jake sun-dried on the deck, he thought of Haven the child and wondered about Haven the woman. He could not connect the smooth, mature drawl of the woman on the phone to the quiet, almost reticent, voice of the child. He knew she had returned home several times over the years. He would see a new model vehicle parked in the same space as her old Toyota used to be. He could only assume it was Haven, although he never saw her, and she was always gone just as quickly as she came. Pulling his shirt over his head, he hurried to the truck, anxious to find out how the years had changed her.

CHAPTER 6

Haven unconsciously slowed her car to an even fifty-five miles per hour, uncharacteristically going the speed limit once she left the last town standing between her and Sugar Bend. Her lead foot had put her well ahead of schedule, and seeing that she was dreading the return in the first place, she sure didn't see any reason to get there early.

The four-lane road narrowed to two, and Haven drove comfortably behind an eighteen-wheeler going even slower than she. A smile interrupted her frown as she thought that any other time she would be anxious for him to hurry up. It seemed she always in a hurry about something, but not today. In fact, she took the time to notice a small gas station off the road to her right that looked more like a clapboard house sitting anonymously on the side of the road. Two rusted pumps were the only reason you knew what it was. She turned on her blinker, ignoring the fact that she had more than enough gas to get to Sugar Bend and halfway back to Sweetgrass before needing to fill up. Crunching to a stop in front of the pumps, Haven opened the door and blinked in the brightness of the spring sun.

"Help you with something, ma'am?" a gravelly voice spoke from behind her. She turned and saw an elderly black man walking crookedly up to her as if each step pained him.

He wore faded blue-jean overalls, one hand hanging limply to his side, with the other tucked into the bib. His white undershirt was stained with sweat and dust, and his dark face bore markings that looked like teeth marks in a Tootsie Roll pop. He wore a red baseball hat that read "Saved in the South."

"No, thank you. I'm just going to get a little gas and be on my way. I see you can't pay at the pump. Do you take credit inside?"

"I never could bring myself to pay that kinda money for them's kinda pumps. Never did trust no machine to get my money right anyway. But I had to let the bank put one of them fancy credit card machines in a while back. Still can't figure out how to use it, though, but I reckon we can get it going if you need to use your plastic. Listen here, you let ol' Clancy pump your gas. Can't have no fancy lady like yourself smelling up thems pretty hands." He took the pump from her before she could protest.

Clancy had heard the soft purr of the car before it ever came to a stop at the pump. In fact, it was the lack of noise that got his attention; the only other cars that ever stopped at his shop were trucks, and they usually came to a shaky stop with a "pop" when the engine backfired. The young lady emerged from the little convertible, long legs bent like that of a spider crawl with one of them cowboy hats that wouldn't last an hour on a real farm. But he could feel the pull on her radiating stronger than gravity. He wondered who or what was doing the pulling.

"You go on inside, out of this heat. I'll be along directly."

For some reason, Haven didn't argue. Although wrinkled up like an unwadded piece of paper, Clancy held an authority that Haven recognized immediately. It reminded her of her father. She took the dusty lot in several strides, unmindful of the dirt collecting on her $300 pair of mules or settling along the hem of her linen skirt.

The door clanged when she pushed it open, revealing a cowbell tied with horsehair twine to the handle. It was a small store consisting of three rows of various groceries such as bread, chips, etc. The floor was bare concrete. The back of the store had refrigerators full of soft drinks, dairy products, and fruit drinks. There were no neon signs advertising beer or alcohol because there was none for sale, Haven noticed. She took a pack of Big Red chewing gum from the candy aisle and peeled off the wrapper. Putting the piece in her mouth, she sat down in one of the three ladder-back chairs that lined the wall facing the dusty parking spaces. It wasn't long before the door clanged open, and Clancy walked in.

"Didn't take much to top you off. You must be killin' time," he said, spitting snuff into a small cup he retrieved from the pocket of his overalls.

"How'd you know?"

"Well, most fancy white girls don't stop at no colored station unless they's about to run out of gas. What's pullin' on you that you be dreading so bad?" he asked wisely, taking the seat beside her.

Haven surprised herself by answering, "I'm not sure which I'm dreading most—going home for going home's sake, or going home because I've got to bury my father."

Clancy seemed to ponder that a minute. "Now that's a shore nuff problem. Home can be tough sometimes, and sometimes it can be the greatest thing for a person. Soothes the soul, sure nuff, but only if you let it. I've lived here all my life; never saw much need to go much anywheres else. Got all I need right here. I don't reckon I'm guaranteed that anywheres else.

"But lettin' someone loves you the way God wanted is tricky. You gotta trust 'em as a child of God. Problem is, folks want to judge folks instead of lovin' 'em like the Lord loves 'em. It's when you love 'em like that, you can take it when theys disappoint you 'cause you know they can't help themselves. We's all sinners, chile. Whacha think 'bout that?"

Haven was a little uncomfortable with the course of the conversation, but considered his thoughts for a moment. "It's an interesting thought, I'll give you that. But what happens when you just lost the only one that ever really loved you?"

Clancy patted her on the knee, using it as support as he winced his way up. "I s'pects you got more folks to love you than you let love you. That's the fool thing about life—we gets so busy and sets in our ways, we forget to let people love us. Sometimes it's hard to take in that much love 'cause then we got to admit we needed it to begin with.

"Well, that's just some crazy old fool talkin'. You from around here?" Clancy asked as he made his way around the counter. Haven followed and placed the gum on the counter as she opened her purse.

"Yes sir, I grew up in Sugar Bend, down by the river. My father was Harry Stunham. He passed away yesterday. I'm here to make arrangements." It was only when she finished her sentence that she realized Clancy was staring at her open-mouthed. Finally, he spoke.

"Sho nuff? You's Harry's chile? Lordy, Lordy, but me and the missus done cried us a river when we heard about Harry leaving us. Just saw him last Sunday at church. Couldn't believe it when I read the paper this morning."

"Did you say church?"

"Why, sho thing. Harry done been worshiping with us down at the All Saints AME just out back. Shoot, I s'pects he been coming to Sunday services since you was a little baby."

Haven shook her head. "I'm sorry. I think you must have my father confused with someone else. My father worked every Sunday at the paper mill. We never attended church."

"You may not have, but he sho did. He sat right in the back pew, never did say much to folks. But I don't think he missed a one. Stood right up at the pulpit a couple of years ago and talked about the redeeming blood of Jesus and how it saved him when his wife done left him. My, my, you must look like your mama 'cause I can't see none of Harry in you." Clancy took Haven's credit card from her outstretched hands. He never noticed them trembling.

Haven stood silent for a moment, slightly embarrassed by being unaware of what was obviously such an important part of Harry's life. She knew he was gone every Sunday without fail. Thinking back, she never remembered him actually saying he was going to work. She just assumed it because he never said anything different. "I don't know what to say. Harry certainly never said anything to me about going to church. I wonder why."

Clancy pulled the paper from the credit card machine and returned Haven's card to her with a pen. "Some folks just private about their fellowship once they gets outside the church. I'm sure Harry didn't want to start no talk 'bout him going to no colored church and all. He was probably protecting you from folks talking," Clancy said with shining eyes.

Haven returned her purse to her shoulder as Clancy came around the counter. A thought suddenly came to her with no provocation. *I don't think much could keep that town from talking.* "Mr. Clancy, would you mind giving me your phone number so that I can let you and your family know about the funeral arrangements?" she asked.

Clancy immediately smiled. "You sure about that? Those white folks might not have a hankering for us coloreds busting up their services. We might have to bring the Holy Spirit with us and really show a worship. Whacha think?" He gave a chuckle.

"Well, if you knew Harry like you said you did, you know exactly what he would say to that. Please, let me call you."

Clancy hastily scribbled a number on the back of Haven's credit card receipt. She placed it in her purse and turned to go. As she reached the door, she stopped and turned. Quickly walking back to Clancy, she reached her arms around his neck and held him tight. She had to reach down to hold him. He just patted the small of her back. She had never been around black people, only Ruby during her childhood, who fully respected her working relationship and never crossed any boundaries with things like goodnight kisses or snuggly bedtime stories. This was the first time a black man, or woman, for that matter, had ever touched her. When she closed her eyes, she could feel her father. "Thank you for being such a good friend to Harry," she said, her words muffled by his shirt.

Clancy just laughed as she pulled away. "Shoot, chile. My wife always tells me, 'The darker the berry, the sweeter the juice.' They don't come much darker or much sweeter than ol' Clancy." Haven gave a wave as she made her way to the car, pulling her sunglasses over her eyes from where they rested on her cowboy hat.

Clancy stared after the little convertible long after the dust settled from her departure. He prayed she'd find her way home.

CHAPTER 7

Haven peeled back the years as easily as peeling a banana when she passed the sign reading "Welcome to Sugar Bend, Home of the Lucky Louis Riverboat Parade" raised above the road like a warning sign, only kudzu now climbed its limbs in its inevitable path toward total world dominance. Her heart skipped a few beats. She lowered herself in her seat, praying for all green lights during the short drive through town. It was a little difficult to be invisible when driving a silver BMW Z4 convertible in a town whose median income never heard of six figures and where government grants kept the city park and graveyards clean. It was as if the few wealthy families in town kept prosperity at the city limits in order to keep their money old. And resented anyone that challenged the unwritten ordinance.

Ruby, the young colored woman that helped around the house in her childhood, would mutter to some of her friends over the phone that the Bishops had started going to that new pediatrician—only she said it softly and slowly as if describing a scene from a pornographic movie.

"I guess they's just too good for Dr. Ketchum; got to get thems a spe-c-i-a-list," she said again slowly. "Shoot. Mae Jean over at the post office says that boy still gets his mail addressed to the 'little white house behind the post office.' I guess that knocks him down a notch or two."

Haven took a moment to reflect on the anomaly that is the South. Although dragging a history filled with tragedy, racism, and violence, the South thumbed its nose at its critics by naming its towns Sugar Bend, Vidalia, and Savannah. Names that rolled off the tongue like lyrics, hoping no one would reflect too long on the composers. *If someone were to give us a plate of crap, we'd just sprinkle a little sugar on top, eat it with our heirloom silver, and bless his heart,* Haven thought.

Stopping at the red light, Haven hit her left blinker, aiming for Marengo Drive, which circumnavigated the town, passing its only funeral home. Jake told Haven that Bobby Downer, the owner of Sugar Bend Legacy, had picked up Harry's body from the hospital and was keeping it until she arrived. Bobby was a third-generation mortician, having survived the scandal of the seventies, in which his father was caught digging up the dead, dumping their bodies in the empty graves, and reusing the caskets, possibly pocketing a few trinkets along the way. It probably would have gone unnoticed if not for the nasty habit of Mallory O'Malley poisoning her husbands.

It was the very good fortune of Mrs. O'Malley's second husband that a routine blood test at his annual physical showed that his wife was slowly killing him with pest control in his morning coffee. Whenever Haven heard the story, it always sounded to her like a limerick,

Mrs. Mallory O'Malley was a good woman. A good woman was she.

She put on a pot of poison. Killing him dead in seventy-three.

It was the not-so-good fortune of Mr. Robert Downer Sr. that the police decided to dig up Mrs. O'Malley's first husband to test him for possible homicide. Imagine the town's surprise when the backhoe dumped a load of dirt from the grave, displaying a very naked and anatomically correct Mr. Johansen beside his empty grave. Mr. Downer was able to pay off the three black men who worked for him digging the holes to take the fall. Because they had no prior records, and the South was progressing in its attempt to level the liability playing field, they were excused with a hefty fine and community service.

Everybody just turned their heads when Mr. Downer paid the fines for the men, saying, "I feel so responsible for trying to help these niggers out by giving them a decent job. I'm so sorry to the family for any grief this may cause." Haven just assumed that everyone forgave the Downers because nobody else wanted to run the funeral parlor, and with a name like Downer, who else would be as qualified? Plus it was the first time Sugar Bend made the state newspapers unless it was about the Lucky Louis Parade.

The light turned green, and Haven turned left past a new flower store on the corner of the highway. The purple wooden sign cheerfully called out Buds and Blooms. Haven noticed a slim brunette sweeping the front walk. She recognized the woman as Roxanne Williams, homecoming queen, head cheerleader, soloist in the choir, and any other accolade fitting the homegrown beauty. She had won a state teen beauty pageant with her tearful response to the question, "How would you best describe your family?" Her mother wasn't even there to hear it, or so the gossips chanted in the school halls. Mrs. Chandler Williams deemed them trashy and unworthy of her attention. Roxanne found out years later that her daddy watched from the far corners of the Montgomery Civic Center, scared to death someone would tell Chandler he'd dared to disobey.

The South searched its small towns to touch a very select few with its wand of importance. Roxanne was one of them. This divine touch, however, often stopped at the physical presence and, more often than not, forgot to place a heart inside its perfect shell. Haven pulled her cowboy hat over her eyes and peered out from beneath it. As if the drive was a presentation of "It's Your Life," Haven was reminded of why she was so reluctant to return home.

Never one to recognize her own beauty, Haven slithered through high school with her back perpetually against a wall and her desk in the back of every class. Growing up with a reticent father on the riverbanks didn't foster any social skills. She was content to keep to herself, study hard, and not buy any trouble with the nickel she didn't have anyway. One day before Christmas break, Haven rounded the corner of lockers and ran straight into Shawn Pruitt, the football quarterback, who was all set to sign with the state university next spring. She rocked back in pain as his elbow caught her just above her right breast and knocked her against the wall.

"Hey, I'm sorry. I didn't even see you there. You okay?" he asked with concern, putting an arm around her shoulders.

Before she had time to respond, a cynical and yet almost lyrical voice wafted up from behind her. "Come now, Shawn. Into wallflowers now, are we?" Roxanne materialized from nowhere with her sidekick, Pam Lyons, smirking snottily over her shoulder. She pulled Shawn's arms from Haven's shoulders and successfully placed herself between them. Her tiny legs escaped the confines of her blue jean miniskirt that Haven knew didn't pass the fingertip rule of the school's dress code. Roxanne seemed oblivious to the fact that it was forty degrees outside. But then again, she was wearing Shawn's letterman jacket. Her teased hair surrounded too much blush on her cheeks, which accented an otherwise perfectly round face.

Barely giving Haven a passing glance, she turned Shawn away, saying, "Come on, honey. I need your opinion on what should be my main focus for the future on my college application. You know how much I need your help, and little ol' me needs all the help I can get if you still want me to go to the same university as you. You still want that, doncha, sugah?" The creator of all things beautiful had also instilled in Roxanne that inner quality of "play dumb and get whatever you want," and even though she didn't invent the tactic, she could go down in the history books as having perfected it. Their voices drifted away, leaving Haven with her mouth open, still holding her books tightly against her stinging chest. Pam Lyons didn't even look back at her as she scurried after her best friend.

As she pushed off the wall, a raspy voice said quietly in her ear, "That just wasn't very nice, was it, Haven?" Ruth was the unofficial town mascot. She was at least forty years old, her straw-colored hair pulled into a ponytail with wisps of gray swirling around her head like pesky flies. She always wore the royal blue wind jacket that Coach Springfield had given her years ago. She walked with an unsteady gait like an old man with arthritic knees. Rumor was her mama dropped her on her head when she was little, granting her an eternal childhood. No one knew her last name or even who her folks were. Or as said in the South, who she "belonged to." She was always at the high school, and most of the time, people left her well enough alone. Never really befriending her, but rarely making fun of her, either. For some reason, she always seemed to gravitate toward Haven. Maybe because she was as mismatched as she.

"No, Ruth, that wasn't very nice. But you and I both know people aren't always very nice," Haven said in return, then put her arm around Ruth's bony shoulders and walked with her out of the building.

"Haven, did you know more people are killed by donkeys than in airplanes?" she asked sincerely as they made their way down the grassy slope separating the two school buildings. Ruth may have been labeled mentally challenged, but she could challenge anyone in a game of Trivial Pursuit. She was a bottomless well of useless facts and would offer them up at any given time.

"No, Ruth, I wasn't aware of that," Haven replied with a smile. Ruth ignored the odd look she received from one of the senior girls whose shoulder she accidentally bumped with her gangly limbs.

"Yup, it's a fact. Did you know that Australia is the only country that is also a continent?"

"That's cool, Ruth. Do you know what a continent is?"

The older lady shook her head rapidly from side to side like a child refusing to take her bedtime medicine. She picked at her fingers, flicking a piece of dried skin onto the concrete walk. She changed the subject before Haven had a chance to tell her.

Haven never knew what had become of her classmates and was surprised to see Roxanne in front of the store. Last she heard she had taken off after Shawn Pruitt to the university, intent on obtaining her MRS. Degree as soon as possible. She never would have pictured her returning to Sugar Bend, unless it was as the grand marshal of the Lucky Louis parade waving to her adoring public with a banner that read "Mrs. Queen of Everything." She drove on, wondering briefly what other changes had occurred in a town that never quite embraced its unlucky and unpretty.

Haven pulled sharply into the empty parking lot and marveled at the gleaming new stucco building in front of her. By the looks of its impressive entry, complete with Grecian columns, potted urns overflowing with Kimberly Queen ferns, and a stamped concrete walk leading up to the front porch, a fatal plague must have descended upon the community for business to be this good. Or else Bobby Downer Jr. returned to the ways of his predecessors and pocketed the family heirlooms of his clients. "Funny thing happened on the way to the cemetery . . ." Haven began singing.

She opened the large mahogany door replicating the state-owned antebellum entryways of so many of the homes around Sugar Bend and was greeted with a blast of cold air. Gentle music flowed from invisible speakers, and a sign on the desk to her right read "Please have a seat. Will return in five minutes." Haven did as she was told and folded into one of the twin love seats that faced each other in the reception area. To her right, she noticed over the faux fireplace a stunning picture of Jesus with His arms outstretched to a group of children. His smile was tender and inviting, and the children seemed to be dancing around His feet. Their faces were painted as if lit up from within rather than from the sun's rays painted high in the sky.

Haven reflected on the inner joy she saw in Clancy. While the skin on his face did not radiate like the children in the painting, his eyes certainly projected that same unbridled joy. *Interesting that two completely different settings—one a hillside of grass under a bright sun, and the other a dusty old gas station—seem to carry that common characteristic*, she thought and left it at that.

She settled back into the comfortable cushions, flipping through a notepad she retrieved from her leather briefcase beside her. The pages held notes regarding the next few days, a six-page checklist ranging from banking business to legal issues such as Harry's will, to preparation of the home to sell. She became so engrossed in her thinking that she didn't hear the faint chime of the front door opening. She never raised her head when Jake blew in.

His long legs took the lobby in several strides, giving Haven the customary passing glance men give to beautiful women. He continued walking several feet toward the back, stopped abruptly, and then turned his head. Sitting over his shoulder was by far the most beautiful woman he had ever seen. His eyes began at her feet, clad in tiny black mules no thicker than a piece of paper, with perfectly painted red toes peeking out of the ends. Her bare legs seemed to go on forever, running into a casual, short linen skirt as if playing peek-a-boo with whoever had the good fortune to admire them. This woman was intense, a slight frown marring an otherwise smooth complexion, oddly pale for this part of the country. He unconsciously stroked his bare chin as he noticed the light hair that escaped the confines of her fashionable cowboy hat and appreciated the slight dusting of freckles that dotted her pale shoulder beneath the white sleeveless blouse. It was those same freckles that he remembered from long ago, and a smile spread across his face.

"Haven?" he ventured carefully, returning to the sitting area. The young woman glanced up from her work, unconsciously smoothing out the wrinkles of her skirt before standing.

"Hello, Jake. Goodness, it's been a long time. Thank you so much for coming," she replied, automatically sticking out her right hand in cool formality. Inside she was anything but cool. In fact, heat spread through her body like molten lava, and an unknown feeling overtook her. Rarely had Haven encountered men that overpowered her physically. Her height often intimidated men. Although Jake didn't tower over her in height, his overall presence consumed the room like a vapor, engulfing every available space for breathing so that Haven was forced to inhale him like the smoke in a burning building. She wasn't used to that.

He was dressed in his usual Levi's, the stress points at the knees standing stark white against the blue threads of his thighs. Haven guessed if he turned around, she would still see the Skoal ring of his youth, hoping he had long since conquered that nasty addiction of dipping tobacco. His boots were the same dusty brown with mud trailing the bottoms, but his blue checkered shirt was neatly tucked into his jeans, and his black, curly hair was still wet, but finger-combed into a presentable state. He was and remained the same raw masculinity that took Haven's breath away during the days before she left for good. She noticed his left hand was bound heavily in gauze, which gave him an aura of vulnerability. And it wasn't until she looked into those same brown eyes that teased her mercilessly in her childhood days, and taught her how to bait a hook, clean a fish, and change a tire that she began to relax.

"You look amazing. I didn't even recognize you, all grown up now. I kept up with you somewhat through Harry. He said you were selling real estate somewhere in Georgia. Must be doing good for yourself. Is that your beamer out front?" Jake hooked his thumbs in the belt loop of his jeans, his weight resting on one hip.

"It pays the bills. But it also keeps me very busy. Not a lot of time for long visits home, unfortunately," she said, tears filling her eyes, as she was jolted back to the reality of the visit. "Do you know where Bobby is? I guess I'll need some suggestions on how we need to proceed."

"Let's hope ol' Bobby Downer's just eating lunch in the back. Hold tight one sec, and I'll run back and see."

Jake shook his head as he retreated down the long, wide hall, viewing rooms lining the way like ant tunnels. He knew there would be some changes in Haven. Everyone grew up at some point, and Haven was about twenty-two years old by his calculations. But man, how do you put so much woman into one body? He recalled his conversation with Brad the other day, speculating on those very changes, strangely content that Haven didn't boast the curves his brother mandated as the minimal worthy of his attention.

Jake found Bobby Downer scarfing down Domino's in the back employee lounge with Miss Stella, the elderly lady who had worked at Sugar Bend Legacy for as long as Jake could remember. She looked like she could qualify as a customer several times over. His mama called her a spinster, although he reminded her no one ever used that word anymore.

"People can choose not to get married, Mama," Jake reminded her.

"I know people can choose not to get married, but the Lord says it's not right for man to be alone. It's right there in His Word, Jake. But Miss Stella's just a little eccentric, that's all. It's got nothing to do with not WANTING to get married," his mama returned.

"She's not eccentric, Mama. She's crazy as a bat. Who in their right mind would have a rooster named Tallulah for a pet, letting it sleep with you on a handmade pillow, and share a bowl of Raisin Bran and a TaB each morning?"

As Bobby returned to his office, Jake watched in amusement as Bobby drooled over Haven while attempting to maintain the posture of an empathetic friend. They went over the details of the reception, scheduled to precede the memorial service on Saturday. All agreed that Harry would haunt them to their own eternity if they had an open-casket viewing.

"One thing I know, Harry wouldn't want anyone looking at him, whether open or closed casket," Haven mentioned.

"Yeah, I figured that as well. What if we did this? Let me and the boys take Harry on down to the graveyard later tomorrow. We'll have a quick reception here early afternoon so everyone can do what we in Sugar Bend do best—give out condolences and congratulations. And then we'll gather in the Magnolia Room for a celebration of life," Bobby suggested. Haven seemed surprised when he mentioned how large the room was.

"I'm sorry, Bobby. I appreciate your suggestion, but given Harry's isolation out there on the river, I don't anticipate we'll have a lot of company. One of your smaller rooms should do just fine," she said pointedly, anticipating an argument based on monetary incentive alone. She seemed experienced in the art of standing her ground, and Jake mentally saluted her seeming inability to be taken advantage of by others.

Bobby looked at Jake questioningly, and Jake just shrugged his shoulders. "Haven, I know you and your daddy were close, but you may not be aware of his involvement in the community the last few years. I can promise you that my suggesting the larger room has nothing to do with squeezing you out of a few more pennies. I'm sincere when I say your daddy will have most of the county and state come to pay their respects. We've already notified the governor."

Jake agreed. "He's right, Haven. Harry surprised us all when he joined ranks with the historic preservation society and successfully fought the state from changing the highway route. They were trying to get it run straight through town to join up with that new bridge, but they would have to tear down the old mill buildings. Harry wouldn't hear of it and made a lot of friends in the process," Jake told her, surprised she didn't know anything about it.

Haven sat back in her chair and folded her hands on her lap, beginning to feel slightly put out by all the secrets that were being revealed about her father. "I do remember his talking about something like that, but Harry was always mumbling about something that I didn't pay it any attention. Sounds like there's a lot more to Harry than maybe any of us realized.

"Okay, Bobby, you win. Show me where to sign. I'll head on home after this and try to find something decent for daddy to wear and run it back up here tomorrow morning. Can I see him now?"

Haven merely raised an eyebrow at Jake when he suggested the blue suit he saw Harry wear when he addressed the state legislature on the importance of preserving historical buildings in Sugar Bend. Bobby suggested running the suit by in the morning.

"On second thought, Haven, would Harry really want to be buried in a suit?" Jake asked.

"Good point, Jake. I'll just get a pair of jeans and his worn-out blue button-down. I know he'd be more comfortable with that," she agreed, beginning to feel annoyed at all the questions that showed how little she really knew of her father.

"Come by before lunch. That would give me about an hour to dress him, so you'd have all the time you wanted before the service . . . . What is it, Jake?" Bobby asked, noticing Jake's stare over his right shoulder.

"Sorry, just admiring your artwork there." Bobby turned in his seat, glancing at a childish drawing of a family of four framed in black on the wall. The mother and two children were outlined with black crayon, fleshed out with a tan color with shoots of grass at their feet. The father, standing just off to the side, was colored neatly and completely in black crayon wearing a red tie with yellow polka dots. Bobby turned back around with a sheepish smile.

"Yeah, well, thanks. It seems as though my son Josh is convinced I'm a black man," he returned. Jake snorted out loud, while Haven put a hand over her mouth to stifle a giggle. "No, it's all right. Laugh all you want. This one's getting a lot of mileage. He came home crying from school, saying he was learning about Martin Luther King and was convinced we couldn't have been friends in the sixties cause I am a black man."

"What's with the picture?" Jake asked.

"He drew that at school as part of his black history month project. The teacher actually hung it on the wall for a week. Cindy had it framed and told me to hang it in my office because it could help with my black constituents," Bobby replied, joining in their laughter. "There might be something to it, though, cause that new colored preacher wants me to meet with his board next week." The three continued laughing for a few minutes, grateful for the respite from the sorrow. As they regrouped, Bobby went through the paperwork with Haven, and the somber mood returned.

After the papers were signed, Jake and Haven said their good-byes, grateful to Bobby Downer for lightening the mood of the afternoon. Haven's spirits lifted slightly having that behind her. They left the building together into the feverish arms of a late Alabama spring.

"Haven, I've got to run by some projects Brad and I've got going on, but I thought I'd scoot by and check on you later this evening before I go home. Would that be all right?" Jake asked, suddenly anxious to be with her, and he hadn't even left yet.

Pleased with Jake's suggestions, Haven glanced back with a nod of her head.

"I would love that, Jake. It seems there's a lot of missing pieces you might can help me put back together. The thought of Harry in a suit alone is enough to warrant the history books. But I don't want to put you out. You must have your own place in town by now."

Jake unconsciously took Haven by the elbow as he led her past his truck to open the door of her car. "No, actually, I decided to make the river cabin my full-time home. Brad's married now. Mom's been dating an engineer over at the paper mill that moved here a couple of years ago. Dad left the cabin to me and Brad, so I just bought his share and moved in. I tell you what. Mom left some casseroles in the freezer for you. How about I pick up some wine, you pick you one out to thaw. We'll cook it up around six o'clock?"

With Haven's acceptance, Jake closed the silver door to her convertible, although she could have easily stepped over the door with her long legs, inconvenient as that would be in a skirt. She waved to Jake over her shoulder as she drove off, turning right onto Marengo Drive. It took Jake a full minute before he thought to move. It was everything he could do to turn left onto the busy road rather than right toward the river and Haven.

Her drive, however, was filled with an uncomfortable nagging feeling that not everything in Sugar Bend was quite as she remembered.

CHAPTER 8

A multicolored parrot greeted Jake as he opened the door to Buds and Blooms with a "helloooo, neighbor!" Jake almost ran into Miss Stella as she made her way out with an armful of freshly cut starburst lilies.

"Do you need any help with that, Miss Stella?"

She was hidden behind the large bouquet. He could just make out the top of her gray head shaking from side to side, and her orthopedic shoes peeked out the bottom of her simple cotton dress.

"No, thank you, Sonny," she replied. "It's Tallulah's birthday. I always bring her seasonal flowers home and cook her a nice steak. I'm running a little behind because that Roxanne took too long." She glanced back with consternation over the top of her horn-rimmed glasses. "Just step aside."

"Oh, okay then. Well, tell Tallulah happy birthday." Jake continued walking through the door, laughing at the "eccentric" older lady, as his mother referred to her.

"Hey, Sinbad," Jake returned to the parrot and glanced around for Roxanne. Not seeing her, he made his way over to the refrigerated closets in the back holding the latest shipment of fresh-cut flowers. In the last few hours, he morphed into the type of man that wanted to bring champagne and flowers to the doorstep of a woman, pour the champagne directly into her mouth, and then drink it while he kissed her deeply. Brad would have a field day with that one for sure!

He couldn't quite explain or begin to articulate the warm feeling that spread through his body when thinking of Haven and would have laughed at the goofy smile that had not left his face since leaving her. If he reflected with a sense of objectivity, he would realize his emotions were completely inappropriate. And yet he could stop the course of his feelings as easily as he could pull a barge with an inner tube. Only he didn't reflect on any of that. He just wanted to buy Haven some flowers.

As he opened the door to the roses, Roxanne appeared from the back, slipping her arms into a pale pink sweater. Her face was a reflection of pain, grimacing as she adjusted the hem. She put a hand on the end of the counter with her head bent as if dizzy from standing too fast. It took her a minute to realize she wasn't alone. She quickly smiled when she saw Jake.

He, however, saw the massive bruising down her right arm before she put on her sweater. It was as if her bully of a husband dipped his hands in black ink and pressed them into her skin. Because Roxanne was so tan, even in the spring, the bruising must be pretty bad to show so clearly. She fussed a little with her hair and strode quickly over to Jake.

"Hey, sugah. I didn't hear you come in. I'll have to get onto Sinbad for not shoutin' a little loudah. What you doin' here at quittin' time? You finally come to your senses and gonna take me away from all my worries?" she asked in typical Roxanne fashion.

Jake and everyone in town knew Mike Thompson beat up on Roxanne on a regular basis. What they didn't know and couldn't figure out was why she put up with it. Jake knew he was a dope dealer, even knew he sold regularly to some of the black kids over in the projects. But every time someone tried to come to her defense, her daddy would lay down like a door mat while her mother walked right over him into the bank board room as majority shareholder and tightened the screws on whoever dared to offer that life wasn't all pretty and perfect. It was like that movie his mama had made him watch all those years ago, *Streetcar Named Desire,* where Blanche Dubois wouldn't let anyone turn up the lights for fear they'd see the reality of her demise.

"Not tonight, Roxanne. You'll have to go on home to Mike," he replied, seeing her visibly wince at his poor attempt at humor. "I need to get some flowers. I don't want to get anything too romantic, but yet something to cheer somebody up. Something happy. I don't know, what do you think? You're the expert."

For a moment, Roxanne looked wistfully at Jake before she replied. "Daisies, honey. Daisies will brighten anyone's mood. Hey, you're not sniffing back around Brigitte again, are you?"

Jake laughed. "No, no, no. Not man enough for that one. Too old and too out of shape. No, Haven Stunham's in town to bury Harry. I thought I'd run her over some flowers to cheer her up."

"Haven Stunham, huh?" Roxanne replied, a coldness creeping into her eyes. "Well, well, well. Flowers for the little wallflower. I'm surprised you're wasting your time on something like that, Jake. You could have any girl in the county, well, anywhere, for that matter. Why do you want to waste your time on that river trash?"

Jake was floored by the sudden change in Roxanne's demeanor. He had known her and countless other women like her to be petty and spiteful. It was almost a rite of passage that young girls develop two faces until they were old enough to decide which one to keep. Obviously, in Roxanne's case, the debate raged on. But always being one to offer the benefit of the doubt, he had chalked Roxanne's history of spitefulness to the unhappiness in her own life. He took a step back and looked at her carefully.

"Now, listen here, Roxanne. I don't know what you've got against Haven, but I've known her a real long time, and there's nothing trashy about her. Not one thing," Jake replied, surprising himself with his tone. He suddenly felt very protective of Haven.

Roxanne began fiddling with the ribbon around a collection of stuffed teddy bears. She tossed her head and turned her back to Jake. "Calm down, calm down. No need to get your feathers ruffled. You always were her little knight in shining armor, weren't you? Not that she ever did anything anyway," Roxanne scoffed back.

"Listen, Roxanne. I know you're going through a tough time now, honey, but there's no reason to take it out on other people, especially someone you haven't seen in a long time. Just say the word, Roxanne, I'll come get you anytime you need me to, you know that. You don't have to stay with someone who's small enough to put his hands on a woman, especially his own woman," Jake said, putting his hand on Roxanne's arm, forgetting about the bruises. She visibly winced under his grip and jerked her arm away.

She ran her fingers through her hair, changing her mood and expression as quickly as if there were an invisible switch at her hairline. "Well, I have absolutely no idea what you're talking about, Jake. Of course you're right about Haven. How just mean of me to hold old grudges for so long. You know she always had the hots for my high school boyfriend. I guess I just never got over that. But, say, let me fix you up a nice bouquet of these daisies with some baby's-breath and greenery. You tell Haven I said hello, ya hear? Will I see her at Brad's party tomorrow night?"

Jake had to forcefully close his gaping mouth as he watched Roxanne once again change expressions. It was just too difficult to keep up. Collecting himself, he played the game. "I'll be sure to tell Haven, Roxanne. Sure is nice of you to say so. We'll see how she feels after the funeral tomorrow about going to Brad's, but she's always welcome." Jake collected the bouquet, paid his bill, and leaned forward to kiss Roxanne on the cheek.

She jerked her head back as if she were slapped when Sinbad cried out, "Helloooo, neighbor" as the store door opened, and her husband slammed through.

Mike stood about six feet, three inches, a solid wall of granite that barreled his way down the Sugar Bend football sidelines, pigskin tucked neatly in his meaty arms like a goodnight teddy bear into the waiting arms of the end zone. Although a few years younger than Jake, he knew even then of Mike's addiction to steroids. It wasn't until he tested positive at the state university that his parents brought him home to work at the family-owned trucking business. He was gone several days out of the week, always coming back meaner than he left. The whole town knew of his return to drugs. But all Roxanne could see when she came home after failing out of college and failing to get a husband was local legend marries local beauty queen. And given the longtime customer relationship with Thompson Trucking and Community Bank and Trust, it was a match everyone anticipated, which in Sugar Bend was so much more important than happily ever after.

Roxanne all but ran toward him, her voice an octave higher than normal. "Well, hey, honey. I wasn't expecting you. What a great surprise! Isn't it, Jake?" She looked pointedly at Jake as she took his arm, her eyes wide with the fear that he would start something.

Mike shrugged her off. "Get your hands off my wife, Baker. I'll tear you up even if you are hurt," Mike growled, coming after him as if he were the fumbled football on an opponent's three-yard line. He stopped just before him. Jake could easily smell the beer on his breath. He seemed juxtaposed, surrounded by stuffed teddy bears holding signs that read "I Love You Beary Much" and cute little chickens titled "Hot Chicks."

"Now, now, Mikey boy. Simmer down. Your wife was just giving me some flowers to take to the second-prettiest girl to return to Sugar Bend. Maybe you heard old man Stunham died yesterday. I'm just taking these to Haven to help cheer her up."

Jake paused for a minute, sizing Mike up quickly with a disgusted look.

"But as soon as we're on a level playing field, anytime you feel the need to beat up on somebody, you come on over. I haven't moved and would much rather you play with me than someone else. Thanks for the flowers, Roxanne. You two be sweet." Jake pivoted on his heel and strode out of the door. His good hand was clenched tightly, itching to take a swing. His breath became shallow as he fought the urge to ruin Mike's otherwise perfectly ugly face with a few bruises to match the ones he put on his wife's arms and God knows where else on her body. He just hoped his friendly peck on the cheek wouldn't cause her more harm.

His blood pressure cooled when his thoughts returned to Haven. Then it raced back up as his thoughts continued with the Haven he met today at the funeral home. His heart pumped all the blood from his head and straight into the parts that women accused men of thinking with all along. *If they only knew how right they were*, Jake thought. He gave a quick laugh as he considered how much alike he and Brad could be.

CHAPTER 9

By habit, Haven pulled her car under the pines, stopping in the same spot she always did growing up as soon as Harry let her drive his rusted Chevy. Putting the car in park and turning off the ignition, she leaned back into her seat and sighed, breathing in the scent of the river. The wet pine straw was holding onto the recent rain, which mixed with the slightly pungent smell of river mud to sting her nose. A hoot owl began its omnipotent waking of the moon, cautioning the sun to wind it up. The smell along with the night sounds called her home as clearly as a mother at dinnertime. It was hard to imagine that she could lock this feeling away every time she blew past the city limits leaving town.

She'd returned a few times following graduation, although not enough to assuage the guilt that filled her now. For a day or two, never three, she and Harry would fall back into their comfortable routine. There would be no special activities like most people plan for visiting relatives. But Haven saw the stress lines in Harry's face relax with each passing hour. And he knew they would return as soon as she left. But something deep within her forced her to always leave first. It was as much a part of her as her heartbeat. Her mother's abandonment taught her she had no control over people's leaving her; she could only control it when she was the one leaving.

The early evening haze exorcised the river gnats that hummed in anticipation of fresh meat. And yet the crickets and occasional deep-throated croaks of the tree frogs called out as if wondering where she'd been. She pictured Harry walking around the side of the house, muttering about how low the river was, how they never could get enough rain when they needed it, too much when it did rain. She glanced at the concrete steps leading up to what most people would consider the front door, anticipating him to lean out and motion for her to hurry up before the bugs got her. Her smile faded and tears formed when she realized she'd never see that again.

It wasn't until Haven collected her suitcase from the trunk of her car that she realized how great the place looked in the setting sunlight. The yard was freshly cut, the shrubs were free of vines, and the pine straw was raked neatly into piles bordering the gravel driveway. *Jake*, she thought to herself. There was no one else she knew who'd go to the trouble.

A rustling sound coming from the box hedges bordering the woods to her left interrupted the ambient noises. Haven dropped her suitcase and, turning her keys into her hand to use as a rudimentary weapon, planted her feet to better face her opponent. All she could make out was something black pointing out from the shrubs, low to the ground. Squinting, she walked carefully toward it, key in hand. The form then lunged at her, surprising her with its agility and speed. She had little time to collect her thoughts.

"Gracie, stop that! It's me, Haven. Come on, Gracie. Come here, girl."

The goose had backed up toward the bushes, fear emulating from her like sweat from a marathon runner. At the sound of Haven's voice, she stopped, lowering her head to the ground.

"Oh, you poor baby. Has anybody been taking care of you? I know you must miss him, girl. Come on, you come with me. We'll get you something to eat." Haven walked around the house, glancing back every few seconds to make sure Gracie was following. She was pleased when she saw the full bucket of food and water by the steps leading up to the deck. She should have known immediately that Jake would have taken care of Gracie, too.

Satisfied, Haven turned her attention to the river in front of her and the vanished daylight. Sometimes twilight fell in a lazy, abstract manner, the dwindling sun brushing the sky like a Georgia O'Keefe painting. And then there were times like this night when the sun hurled dusk toward earth as if the day was just too big a burden to carry anymore.

But Haven didn't need any light to know the path that would lead her to the water. The air was heavy and thick, occasionally stirred by a stingy breeze. She'd often tell Harry on nights like this she could scoop up the night air with a spoon and eat it for supper. There were no noises, save the crickets, and they were mostly quiet. The grass was chopped up and hard, more natural groundcover than the Bermuda out in front of the house. The woods broadened until falling off into the river, and wild Cherokee rose bushes dotted in and out of the pines. Haven breathed in their scent, drawing strength from their history. It was a history Harry shared with her as a young girl when he caught her picking the blooms one summer afternoon.

"Thems plants here for a reason, girl," he said roughly, taking the blooms from her hand. He let her know their home was in the direct path of the Trail of Tears, a reluctant and solemn walk in the 1830s in which thousands of Cherokee Indians who steadfastly refused to leave their homes were forcibly removed by the United States government. Men, women, and children dragged along thousands of miles, leaving their heritage and culture behind them—traveling along a dusty trail patted down with fallen tears. A lot didn't survive; many more wished they didn't. In desperation, the elders cried out to the Heaven Dweller to have mercy on their women, for they knew the children would draw strength from them. And that strength was paramount to the continuance of their culture.

"The Heaven Dweller told her children to wake in the morning. There'd be a sign," Harry said. "And when they woke, there were Cherokee rose bushes everywhere an Indian tear had fell."

Harry took the last rose Haven held in her hand. "See here at these five petals. They're the five tribes of the Cherokee. And the Heaven Dweller made the vines with stickers so the white man couldn't tear 'em down with his bare hands. And those women got the strength they needed to press on. Don't take away that strength, Haven. Don't ever take nothin' that ain't yours."

It was the strength of the river that guided her footsteps now. It pulled her as strongly as the moon crafts ocean waves, taking placid, distant saltwater and rolling it to the shore. She was renewed with each breath and drank it through her eyes until they overflowed in tears down her cheeks.

She always experienced revival in the moonlit ribbon of water that curled around the chewed-up corners of earth. She preferred the nighttime waters to the daylight river she would have to share with others. She entered it as reverently and anonymously as a confessional. This dark, inky, and undisturbed refuge held Haven in her arms, never allowing her to be afraid of the life that swam inside her womb. The Spanish moss that hung from her trees dripped like tissue ready to dry her tears of loneliness in adolescence, never getting on to her when she shared her feelings of isolation. And the river baptized her with acceptance when she said her final good-bye, understanding that the bond between the two would be carried forward no matter where Haven laid her head. It could do so knowing the water's pull eventually would bring her home.

Haven kicked off her shoes and walked barefoot toward the river, shedding clothes along the way. Gracie followed her, cautiously at first, then more quickly as Haven's pace picked up. When she reached the wooden dock, she spread her arms wide, bathing herself in the now present moonlight that wrapped its arms around her. She walked to the edge of the dock, her toes touching the tires haphazardly stapled around the dock to serve as a bumper. She spun around, keeping her arms outright, chin up to the stars that blinked a surprised hello. Tears coursed down her cheeks, realizing then that she owed as much to the river as she did to Harry—maybe more because she was always the same. She was always here. There were no surprises. Dizzy, she lifted her hands over her head and fell into the water, submerging herself in familiarity and wondering if she'd have the strength to come back up.

Haven was sitting on the back deck clad only in a pair of cutoff shorts and Harry's red plaid shirt that was surprisingly clean. Her long hair was still damp, splayed across her shoulders like chafed wheat after a rain. Her peripheral glance took in a single light rounding the bend, and she continued sitting in silence as the boat made its way to the dock. A tall figure emerged, tying the rope to the anchor. Jake gave a salute as he made his way up the darkened path, as Haven had yet to put on a light. Her suitcase remained by her car in the front.

Jake became concerned as he approached the house; the figure on the porch had not moved. He wouldn't be confident it was Haven if the moonlight was not so bright against her pale hair. "Haven, you okay?" he asked as he placed his right hand on the wooden rail and walked up the steps carrying a bottle of wine and the bouquet of daisies.

Haven's eyes cleared as if woken from a dream. The ice in her glass of tea clinked as she raised it to her lips for a small sip. Condensation dripped into her lap. "Hey, Jake. Sorry, I guess I was a little lost in thought. Are those flowers for me? Please come on up and have a seat. I'll find something to put them in."

Jake touched her on the shoulder when he approached, much more comfortable with the Haven before him in her bare feet and cutoffs than the sophisticated city girl he met that afternoon. "No, don't get up. Let me just put this wine in the refrigerator to keep it chilled. I'll find something to put the flowers in. Do you mind if I get a glass of tea?"

Haven placed her hand over his and said, "Don't be silly. This is as much your home as it is mine."

Jake left her reluctantly, still unsettled by her monotone and weariness. He opened the back screen door and walked into the kitchen. The house was dark, so he switched on the kitchen light and placed the chardonnay into the fridge. He noticed the oven had not been preheated, nor did he see any sign that she had defrosted a casserole. Glancing through the kitchen window, he saw that Haven still had not moved. He pulled a plastic dish from the freezer marked "chicken/rice" in his mother's handwriting and stuck it in the microwave to defrost while turning on the oven. After taking care of a few more things, he got a tumbler out of the cabinet, poured a glass of tea, and returned to the deck.

They sat in silence for a while, content to let the night sounds fall around them. The air had a slight dewy feel as if warning of a coming rain. Haven was the first to break the silence.

"I want to thank you, Jake, for all you did for Harry. I hated leaving him here by himself. I probably wouldn't have done it if I weren't confident you'd be around to help him. It upsets me to think of him here by himself, alone, with no one to talk to. But at least I never had to worry about him having to take care of this place by himself, and for that, I'm grateful."

Jake leaned back into the wooden rocking chair, gently swaying back and forth. "You don't have to thank me, Haven. You all been like family to me. Harry was real good to my mama when Daddy died. I know you don't know about that because you weren't born. But he came over and cut our grass, unstopped a few toilets, that sort of thing. He always made sure our river cabin was all right, patching a few shingles along the way. Brad and I always swore, although Mama would have made sure of it anyway, that we'd return the favor when we could. It was just easier for me because of being at the river all the time. Brad was always with his wife, Beth, by that time. Plus, I really enjoyed old Harry. He was actually pretty fun to be around once he quit trying to be so mean.

"Did you know he's the one that taught me and Brad to shoot a gun?" Haven shook her head without lifting it from the rocking chair.

"I'll never forget how excited we were," Jake said, beginning the story.

Jake was about eight years old; Brad eleven. It was an early, way-early, winter Saturday morning when their mother roused them from their bunk beds.

"Get up, babies. Mama's got breakfast ready, and Mr. Harry'll be along shortly," she said, shaking the mounds under the feather comforters.

"Harry who?" Brad mumbled under the covers. Jake merely rolled over.

"What do you mean, Harry who? Harry Stunham. He's bound and determined to teach you guys to shoot a gun so I s'pect he's on his way now to pick you up."

That was all they needed to hear. Just last week the boys had listened to Dickie McKenzie brag about bagging a deer. He told them his daddy put deer blood all over his face.

And he had the Polaroid picture to prove it. There he was, as big around as he was tall, smiling gap-toothed into the camera. He was kneeling beside an eight-point buck with its blood smeared across his face like war paint. Jake gave it nonchalantly back to him while choking down a big ol' wad of envy. The boys threw off their covers and threw on some clothes, both sucking in their breath as their bare feet hit the icy hardwood floor. Not fifteen minutes later, a pancake in each hand, the boys loaded up in Harry's pick-up. They drove back out to the river as the sun was rising.

"Why ain't we goin' to your place, Mr. Harry?" Brad asked when Harry turned into the Baker's dirt driveway that looked more like a worn path through the trees.

"A man should learn how to take care of his own property, not somebody else's. Ya boys'll learn how to shoot on yer own land. Plus I don't want the baby runnin' after us." Harry returned, a smile tugging at his mouth as Jake dug some sleep out of the corner of his eye.

"Where is Haven?" Jake asked as the truck crawled into a small clearing just off from the river house. The sound of the truck door slamming hung in the thick air. Leaving the truck, they made crunching sounds with their boots, the ground not yet soft under the rising sun. The pines stood tall and bare like thin soldiers guarding a secret. The only sound was a wren and a squirrel, fussing like an old married couple.

Brad nudged Jake with his elbow and acted like he was smoking a cigarette, his breath coming out in smoky waves in the cold November morning. Jake laughed. Not because he thought it was funny, but because he was nervous...or excited...probably both.

"Ruby's got her," was all Harry offered.

He'd placed a target not 25 yards from a fallen log with a dirt mound at its back. He carried a shotgun and a box of shells.

All three sat on the log, a boy on each side of Harry. "This here's a 22 caliber rifle. It's the kinda gun your daddy woulda bought ya if he were still alive. C'mere and let me show it to ya." He showed them the barrel; let them feel the smooth wood of the stock. His bony fingers broke the gun down, meticulously teaching every part in respect to its purpose. He showed them how to load the rounds in the magazine; how to make sure the chamber was empty. He was clear and precise in teaching them to never walk with a round in the chamber and to never carry a loaded gun into a house. If he said it once, Jake remembered him saying it a hundred times that.

"Always put away an empty gun," he emphasized. "When yer usin' it, it's okay to carry it with rounds in the magazine. But never put a round in the chamber unless yer ready to shoot it. This here gun could be a dangerous thing if ya don't respect it. When ya do, then you'll only use it the way God intended fer ya to."

The gun trembled in Jake's hand, or maybe it was the other way around. Harry let Brad feel it first then Jake. But Jake was more reluctant to let it go. The boys learned how to load the gun, then practiced walking with it always ensuring the safety was on and the barrel pointed to the ground. They practiced sighting the gun and swinging it to view different objects. Jake instinctively placed the stock of the gun correctly into the turn of his shoulder as if it were a missing limb. He stood in reverence as the wood molded into his skin, creating another layer of derma, warming his purple hands. His pulse seemed to pump his blood through his arm, permeating the wood of the stock, down the barrel and warming his body through his fingertips.

"Did you ever get to shoot?" Haven asked.

"Eventually, but not until we had mastered how to take care of it. I bet we cleaned that gun a hundred times before he was satisfied. Harry said you didn't earn the privilege of enjoying something until you learned how to take care of it. I'll never forget the scripture he told us from memory, then made us learn it. It was from Psalm chapter 65: 'You care for the land and water it; You enrich it abundantly. The streams of God are filled with water to provide the people with grain, for so You have ordained it.'

"I keep that scripture in my truck, not that I could forget it. Harry taught me that we have a responsibility not only to the land, but also to each other. And Mama taught me that when we take care of each other we find joy and with that joy comes Jesus," Jake said.

"It's strange to hear stuff like that. You're talking about a Harry I don't even know. He never talked to me about God or religion. I never even knew he had a Bible. I wonder why he could talk to other people, but not to his own daughter," Haven said.

Jake considered that a minute. "I bet he showed it to you in a million ways; you just had to know where to look. I've learned that sometimes Jesus is quiet, but He's still there if we look for Him. I find Him mostly when I'm fishing. Mama finds Him when she's doing her baking or serving on some committee. I believe Harry felt more comfortable talking to us boys about his faith, but maybe more comfortable in just showing it to you."

Haven pondered that a minute, then spoke.

"I didn't realize ya'll spent that much time together," Haven replied, mirroring Jake's repose in her own rocking chair beside him. "You must have known my mama then."

Jake nodded. "I remember what she looked like. I remember Mama talking about her leaving to some of her buddies. But I don't know any more than you do probably. Harry never talked about much. Unless he talked about you, he just complained or moaned about something that wasn't going right. He spent a lot of time riled up about the state tearing up the mill buildings, I can tell you that."

"Tell me what you remember about her," Haven implored, refusing to change the subject. "Harry never told me anything except that she couldn't handle being a mama, and it was a good thing that she left when she did. He never seemed mad. Maybe just a little sad is all. And Ruby would always say I would find out when I found out. That was real comforting to a five-year-old," she replied with a sarcastic snort.

"Yeah, that sounds like Ruby. Your daddy sure was lucky to find her, even if she didn't always say the right things. You couldn't ask for anybody better to help raise you. Whatever happened to Ruby?" Jake asked.

"She moved back to Atlanta when I started high school. We get letters from time to time. I write back every once in a while. I think she's doing okay. She must be about seventy by now.

"But don't go changing the subject. Tell me about my mama. What did she look like? Do you know I've never even seen a picture?"

Jake looked at her carefully, never realizing until now just how much Haven missed by not having a mother to think that each and every drawing she did in preschool was of Rembrandt quality, every visit to the batter's box was a home run, or every school picture taken would be framed on the wall despite the missing teeth or the chunk of hair cut out to get rid of gum.

"I remember how beautiful she was. She had this amazing hair, just like yours could be if you ever bothered to fix it. I remember one time I had to run over to get Harry when I spotted a bed of cottonmouths. I guess I was about six. Mama wouldn't come out of the house because of the snakes. I ran down the dirt road as fast as I could, scared to death like little boys feel when they see snakes. I didn't see Harry, so I ran around the house and saw Miss Belle sitting down at the dock. It just hit me that she was pregnant with you."

Jake described her to Haven. She was wearing a white nightgown with no sleeves. Jake remembered he could see right through it. It almost looked like a choir robe it was so loose around her big stomach. She was sitting cross-legged, looking up at the sky with her eyes closed. She looked like an angel because her skin was so white. But she was crying. She wasn't sobbing. Didn't really make a sound at all. But the tears were coming down her face like she was. And she was so still that if it weren't for her sitting up, Jake would have sworn she was dead. It was the only time he saw her.

"Why was she so sad?" Haven asked.

"I have no idea. I remember hearing Mama say that Belle Stunham never did take to the river. Apparently, she was from up north somewhere. Harry met her when he went to some training or something for the paper mill. Married her and brought her back before anyone knew what was going on. Must have gotten pregnant right away because she didn't stay here long."

"I was six weeks old. At least he told me that much. But he never would tell me why. Would always say, 'People got to find their own joy, Haven. Not everybody gonna find it in the river like we do.' It always bothered me that she could have some mental condition that I don't know about. What if she has some sort of disease that could be passed down?" Haven's voice grew louder in agitation as she questioned Jake.

Jake reached over and placed his hand over hers. "Haven, think about it. We both know Harry had his faults, but he was an honorable man. If there were something you needed to know, he woulda let you know. Remembering her now reminds me of how much you look like her. That couldn't have been easy on him, just like it wasn't easy on you growing up without a mama. But we all try to do the best we can do. Just remember that. He's right about finding your own joy. You can't make it for them.

"Let me tell you this, too, Haven. Harry talked to me several months after you left. He told me to make sure you understood how much he loved you. He said he was never good at the emotional stuff. But he specifically told me to look after you. Not that you can't look after yourself. In fact, he was proud he raised you that way. But it was more about to make sure you knew how to be happy. How to love. I'd like to keep my promise to him and be with you this weekend at least. Do you mind if I stick around?"

Haven sat quietly in the dark, keeping her tears inside so as not to have to share with Jake just yet. Joy. Did she have it? She sure felt something out here on the river. It was almost spiritual, but that couldn't be right. All she'd ever known about the spiritual was when Ruby had on that preaching on the radio. Some deep voice screaming and yelling about getting right with God so you could build your mansions in heaven. She never knew what getting right meant. How did you get wrong to begin with? It all sounded like an awful lot of work to Haven. She'd rather put her energy into her career. Make something of herself. Stand out in a way that she could control instead of standing out for reasons she couldn't.

Jake just listened to the silence.

While she was as comfortable with Jake as ever, the years that had passed caused her to fall back on her safety net of reticence. She waited until she had control in her voice before she spoke.

And Jake let her.

"No, of course not, Jake. I'm grateful for all you've done. I haven't even unpacked. I haven't really looked around the house, but I did see how cleaned up it is and got here early enough to see the yard's been kept up. I really appreciate that. I know Harry would, too."

"I can't take credit for the house. You know southern Methodists. As soon as Mama and her church group found out about Harry, they whipped out their aprons, threw together a few casseroles and sweet tea, and marched out here, armed with mops and dustpans, before Harry left the emergency room. Speaking of casseroles, I set one out to thaw. I'll run inside and heat us up some chicken and rice and open that bottle of wine. Here, let me take your glass," he said, reaching for her empty tumbler.

Haven laughed at Jake's description of his mama. "Let me at least help, Jake. I'm sorry I forgot about defrosting dinner. I guess I just got caught up in memories. Something about the river makes me lose time. Harry always used to say he was going to move my bed down to the dock 'cause it was breaking his back having to carry me up to the house after I fell asleep on the dock." She pushed up from her chair, and the two made their way inside to begin dinner.

Haven had to smile to herself as she noticed the masking tape on the bottom of the Tupperware serving dishes. In black probably permanent maker read the name and address of its contributor. Southern Methodists always gave with whole hearts while fully expecting the appropriate thank you note. To them, even death did not preempt the practice of proper manners. Haven got her notebook from her briefcase, which had mysteriously appeared by the kitchen table, along with her suitcase and began making a list.

The two sat down to dinner. The smell of chicken and pepper circled around Haven's nose, and she realized she hadn't eaten all day.

"Tell me about Brad. You said he was married. I can't believe there's a girl alive that could tame Brad Baker," Haven said while chewing, her elbows on the table and fork dangling from her hand.

"You haven't met Beth, yet. She's not from here. She lived in Cedar Falls, just up the river, but covered this and several other counties as a social worker. That's how she met Brad," Jake replied, taking a sip of wine. "Believe it or not, Brad joined up with the Big Brother/Big Sister program at the YMCA and became a big brother to DeJesus, a Mexican about five years old at the time. He was in a bad way. Never knew his daddy. Mama strung out on drugs. And yet he kept coming around the Y, shooting basketballs by himself. Never bothering anyone.

"Brad and I used to go play racquetball. We kept noticing DeJesus. Brad asked Matt Taylor about him. Do you remember Matt?"

Haven nodded, her mouth full. Jake continued, "Well, Matt told Brad all about him, how he never saw his family. How DeJesus barely said anything to anyone. How he even caught him going through the garbage to get a bag of chips somebody didn't finish. He was so thin you could count every bone of his ribs. And big boy Brad just went to pieces. I mean cried like a baby. As soon as he got ahold of himself, he and Matt formed a plan, and next thing you know, they had DeJesus' mom in his office, sober enough to sign the papers for him to join the program. Brad became his big brother."

"How does Beth fit in?" Haven asked, finishing her glass of wine and generously pouring herself another. Jake lifted his glass to indicate a refill before he continued.

"Like I said, Beth was a social worker who was assigned DeJesus' case because he ended up in the emergency room with a broken arm. Brad was the one who brought him in. Social Services was automatically contacted because of the nature of the injury. If you can believe this, Brad was actually listed as a suspect. Beth interviewed him when she first took the case."

Jake began laughing so hard he doubled over, clutching his stomach.

"I don't see anything funny about that," Haven replied, taking offense at Jake's twisted sense of humor.

Jake collected himself, wiping the tears from his eyes as his laughter died down. "Naw, it wasn't at the time. But looking back, it was a hoot to see little ol' Beth giving Brad the business. She was just doing her job, but Brad was so bothered about the whole thing, he would sull up like a baby girl who won't eat her vegetables whenever Beth came around. Needless to say, it didn't take long for those two to put that energy to better use. They got married about six months later. They are now the official foster parents of DeJesus 'cause his mother is in jail. She let one of her boyfriends beat on that little boy. You'll meet him at Brad's party. He's been heaped on with so much love you'd never know all he went through to get to this place. Of course, Mama just eats him up and can't cook fast enough for him."

Haven sat quietly for a moment, finishing the last bites of her dinner.

"Let me ask you something, Jake. Did you know Harry worshiped every Sunday at that colored church just outside of town?"

Jake shook his head. "Can't say for sure, but I knew he always disappeared on Sundays. Doesn't surprise me, though. Harry was a spiritual man. He was always reading his Bible down by the river. I'd see him most mornings whenever I'd come by fishing. Why's that?"

Haven told him about meeting Clancy and calling him earlier to invite him to Harry's services that weekend.

"Old Clancy Rutledge. I just knew he'd be dead by now. He must be ninety. He used to give me a nickel whenever I'd catch him at the hardware store in town. It's good to know he's doing well. I didn't realize he opened that gas station."

"Do you think I'll get the gossip mill going by inviting his family to Harry's services?"

Jake thought for a minute. "You know, this town always surprises me. Just when I think I've figured it out, it goes and does just the opposite. But even if it does, at least it will get folks talking. And even better, get them talking to each other."

They discussed the segregation that still existed in the South, although now more out of conformity than any mandate. Folks just always doing what they've always done, they reflected to each other, rather than venturing beyond past experiences. And that the natural segregation existed on both sides.

"I'm not talking racism. That's an entirely different matter. I'm talking about how blacks tend to sit with blacks in the school lunchroom, or how whites tend to worship only in white churches. Or that you can still tell the difference in a church by whites or blacks. Do you know the high school still elects black and white homecoming maids? Hard to believe.

"It's kind of like taking the same way to the grocery store every time because it fits into your schedule. But one day you come to a detour because of roadwork or something and realize you've missed out on the prettiest drive in town because of taking the same road out of habit. Does that make sense?" Jake asked, getting up to collect the dishes.

Haven nodded sleepily at Jake. Her full stomach following the meal did not keep her head from feeling fuzzy. The empty bottle of wine fused her thoughts together as one and caused her words to travel over a seemingly swollen tongue. It was late, and she was tired. As he cleared the table, Jake noticed her hiding a yawn behind her hands.

"Haven, I'm going to head on home, unless you want me to bunk here on the couch. You've got a long weekend ahead of you and need your sleep. What time do you want to go over to the funeral home to take Harry's suit tomorrow?"

After making their plans and accepting her assurances that she was okay, Jake let himself out the door and made his way down to his boat. Haven locked the door behind him, and then unlocked it. She realized that never in her childhood had a door been locked in this home. She patted the door as if stroking the family pet and leaned her head against its pane. There were no more tears left to come, only the desire to sleep in Harry's bed, wrapped up in his smells, and let him somehow realize that although she didn't know joy or whether or not she was happy, she did know he did the best he could do. With that realization came a tiny fragment of desire for all the things she never knew were missing.

CHAPTER 10

The morning dawned gray and gloomy, causing Haven to smile despite the slight headache forming between her eyes. She could just imagine Harry in heaven, stomping up to God in what she now recognized as his good "speech" suit and giving a word or two about the chance of rain on his parade. She had awakened at dawn, automatically retreating back to the days when daylight marked half a day gone in Harry's world. She tended to a few chores, made sure Gracie was fed and watered, then prepared for the day.

She had returned to the rocking chairs from the night before wearing only Harry's robe and an old pair of his tube socks. The robe fell loosely about her shoulders as the rising sun warmed her skin. She raised her coffee mug in salute to the water, whispering good morning as a gentle breeze stirred the pine branches as if they were stretching their arms from a good night's sleep. After more than an hour of simply nothing, Haven returned to get ready for the day she didn't seem to be dreading quite so badly.

Following a leisurely bath and simple grooming, Haven stood in front of an armoire in Harry's sparsely furnished room. That and a brass bed were its only occupants. She brushed away lint that wasn't really there on Harry's shirt, busying her hands while waiting for Jake to pick her up. She had dressed in what she called her staple black dress with straps that tied around her neck and a plunging neckline that she took no notice of due to the fact there was not much to notice in that area. She made her way outside when she heard the approaching tires crunching along the drive.

Jake became uncomfortable again when he saw Haven, still unable to grasp that this tall drink of sophistication was the Haven of his adolescence. Her hair was pulled into a French twist, small tendrils twirling around her ears like ballerinas in a pirouette. The black dress was in contrast with her pale skin, and yet he could see those freckles splashed across her chest leading down the neckline like the points on a map to a buried treasure. He shifted in his seat, pulling on the knot in his tie to allow more breathing room, and then cursed his curly black hair for its unruliness. He jumped out of the truck and ran to the other side.

"Did you sleep okay?" he asked, feeling like a kid on his first date instead of a grown man taking a woman to her father's funeral.

"Good as can be expected, I guess. I saw Harry's speech suit and am still having a hard time imagining him in it, giving the state legislature the business. I bet he looked handsome. It's funny. I don't think I've ever seen him in a suit." Haven was reluctant to admit that Harry's involvement in state politics wasn't the only thing she was having a hard time reconciling in her mind. As the weekend progressed and against her wishes, Sugar Bend itself began to soften around the edges.

On the ride into town, Jake regaled Haven with stories of her father and his fight for historical preservation. Haven smiled when hearing about Harry's sitting outside a senator's office, all but accosting him on his way to lunch. The story about how he and several others organized protests on the riverbanks, which actually turned out to be a festival because the old folks brought their banjos and harmonicas, made her laugh out loud. He made sure all the right people were invited to the Lucky Louis Riverboat Parade that fall so they could see the value in keeping the highway away from the river. Jake enjoyed telling the tales, encouraged by Haven's laughter.

"What's going on with the old bridge?" Haven inquired as they slowed down to allow a tractor to back onto the road, to align itself with its ditch, and to move forward again over the embankment. She had not noticed all the heavy equipment when she rode over the night before.

"Well, the government has finally gotten off its asher and is building a new bridge . . . ." Jake trailed off when Haven interrupted him.

"I'm sorry, did you say asher?"

"Yeah, sorry. Another one of my made-up cuss words. You remember that Mama never would let us cuss. Old habits die hard, I guess," Jake replied.

Haven gave a soft chuckle, "I had forgotten all about that. Asher, huh?"

Jake laughed with her. "Well, like I was saying, the government said it will take a couple of years, and if the government has anything to do with it, you can add a couple of years onto their couple of years. But the good news is at some time in the future, Sugar Bend will have a celebration when we blow up that old bridge. They're talking about bringing in some sort of detonation expert so that we can have a party on the riverbank and watch the bridge explode. I tell you what, I'll be first in line to push the button, that's for sure," he said with passion.

Haven touched his arm with sympathy, remembering his father's death. Jake enjoyed the feel of her hand and was pleased when she kept it there, unconsciously stroking his arm with her thumb. They drove on in silence along the oak-lined streets of town, stopping at the four-way stop at the corner of Main and Broad. He was almost sorry to pull into the parking lot of the funeral home.

The meeting with Bobby went quickly, confirming the announcement in the morning's paper, although word of mouth was much quicker than any formal media announcement. Although the governor declined attendance due to calendar conflicts, two state senators and the house speaker would be attending the visitation and memorial service. While Haven had no other family, she quickly realized her father was like family to many.

Jake was impressed with Bobby's ability to look serene while calculating the charges for such a large funeral. His graying hair was oiled into a comb-over, and his charcoal suit was one size too small. Jake could just detect a small smile as Haven coolly wrote him a check, once again thanking him for all his assistance.

"We all loved Harry, Haven. It is my pleasure. Let's see," he said, glancing at his gold Rolex watch on his beefy left wrist, "We've got a while before the reception. Give me about an hour and then you're welcome to come spend time with Harry before all the people arrive."

"Thank you, Bobby. I definitely want to do that. Maybe we can run and get something to eat and be back then?" She directed the question to Jake, who nodded.

Walking back to the truck, Jake put his arm casually around Haven's shoulders. "Mama really wants us to come by for lunch. I meant to mention it last night and forgot. Do you feel like being around others?"

She really did not, never having been comfortable in a crowd, much less a crowded family. But how could she say no after all they had done? "Of course. That sounds wonderful. I only hate I don't have anything to bring."

"You'd only insult her if you did," he replied, opening the door and holding her elbow as she stepped into the truck.

He could hear her cell phone ringing as he climbed in the other side and started the engine.

Haven retrieved her phone from her purse and pressed the button. Before she could speak, Mark's voice came over the line.

"Hey, sweet nips. Uncle Mark was worried about his little chicken and wanted to see how things were progressing in Redneckville. Ya'll strung anybody over a tree yet? Need me to call up ol' Atticus?" Mark loved teasing Haven about her small-town origins and often quoted books like *To Kill a Mockingbird.*

"Oh, Mark. I'm so glad to hear from you," Haven replied, mouthing Jake an apology. "I am doing fine. I'm riding with Jake Baker, who was a good friend of my father's. He's helping me take care of things. How are things going at work?" She didn't notice Jake's slight frown when she only mentioned his relationship with Harry. It seemed almost deliberate to him.

"I refuse to talk about work to you while you are in mourning. That is just gaudy, and my mother raised me better. She couldn't keep me from being gay, but she certainly taught me proper etiquette. Maybe that's what did it! If she realized how much I enjoyed those lessons, she might have spent less time on cotillion and more on Little League!" he said laughing in his feminine voice and fussing with his hair in the rearview mirror of his Porsche.

Haven couldn't resist joining him in laughter as she thought about Mark's mother. She was as round as she was tall, white hair perfectly coiffed and pearls on her ears, neck, and wrist. Her jewelry was always too tight, like the division between link sausages. But she flitted around Mark, never admitting to herself his sexual orientation and yet thrilled when he took her antique shopping or manicured her nails as a young boy.

Haven hung up the phone after promising to call following the funeral. "I'm sorry, Jake. That was a great friend of mine that has picked up a lot of my slack at work this past week."

"Don't worry about that. He made you laugh, that's what's important," Jake replied, surprised at the sharpness of his tone. If he had been willing to admit it, there was a twinge of jealousy to his words.

Haven was surprised by his tone and continued staring at the road, wondering how she could have offended him.

Jake continued the silence, embarrassed by the way the soft sound of her voice while talking to another man made him feel. The past few days had awakened a sense of protectiveness in him that he didn't know existed.

Finally, Haven spoke. "Mark's been one of my best friends for the past few years. He's been my escort to most functions around Sweetgrass. He's a safe date because he's been out of the closet his entire life. Although I don't understand his lifestyle, Mark has a pure heart."

"Oh, well," Jake stuttered, completely caught off guard and further embarrassed by his behavior.

"Don't worry, I'd never expose him to Sugar Bend. But he and Lila are the best friends I've ever had," she replied. "I know we were raised that homosexuality is wrong, but it's hard for me to judge him. I know he goes to church and is searching for a place that will accept him for who he is. Or at least show him another way to be. But honestly, I don't know what I would do without Mark. He's my official furniture mover and picture hanger."

Jake considered her words for a minute and then sighed. "I don't know, Haven. The older I get, the more I realize folks just gotta figure out for themselves what's right or wrong when it comes to the Lord. I guess I just got too many warts to be showing other folks theirs. I don't figure it's my job to convict them. Who's this Lila?" Jake asked, changing the subject.

Haven spent the remainder of the drive to the Bakers' telling Jake about Lila. It was difficult to describe her, just like a writer would struggle to define life. Life is so subjective to its interpreter, and so was Lila Adams. But he laughed at her stories, and the two returned to that comfortable place of the night before.

In all the years she'd known Jake, she'd never been to his home, but it was exactly as she imagined it. The mostly ranch houses on the tree-lined street were so close together you could borrow a cup of sugar by sticking your hand out of a window. The Baker home was a small brick cottage, painted white with four thick columns lining the front porch. It had a low-slung roof that Haven could probably touch on her tiptoes walking up the front steps. The porch looked like an outdoor living area, one end complete with a black wicker settee adorned with brightly colored pillows in colors of fuchsia, green, and black on the right side. Flanking it were two urns with small crepe myrtle trees and lantana with trailing ivy. To her left was a dining area with a black wrought iron table shadowed by a low-hanging candle chandelier. An heirloom vase stood in the center with several majestic irises in purple. Potted impatiens lined the railings and color burst in visual jubilation wherever the eye wandered. Jake seemed to take it all for granted and was several steps ahead of Haven before he realized she didn't follow.

"You okay?" he asked, coming back to take her elbow.

"I'm fine. I'm just overwhelmed by how beautiful everything is. Your mother's very talented. I can only imagine how the rest of the house looks."

"Yeah, she spends a lot of time on her flowers. I think that's why she waited so long to start dating again. Daddy was dead about thirteen years before she went out on her first date. But she kept herself busy."

The door opened before Jake could turn the knob, and Haven was instantly enveloped in a warm hug that smelled like flour and cinnamon.

"You sweet girl. Come here and let Mrs. Baker love on you. You lean on me, honey, and not on your own understanding. Come on in this house, now. You come on in with me. Jake, shut the door before you let all the bought air out and all the bugs in." Marianne Baker was the definitive mother, an ample waistline needed to house such a big heart. She walked with her head slightly bent, eyebrows perpetually raised to give her view over her black-framed bifocals. Haven couldn't help but let her guide her in the house, all the while fussing over how beautiful she was, but she was too skinny and needed fattening up, and who does she have to cook for her, and so on. Marianne talked with one long sentence. Jake just shrugged with a smile as Haven looked at him imploringly over her shoulder.

The hour flew by, as people rushed in and out of the little house. Haven was reunited with Jake's brother, Brad, who gave Jake thumbs up while giving her a hug in welcome. Jake merely rolled his eyes in response. She briefly met Brad's wife, Beth, who apologized for not staying, but whispered conspiratorially that she was just too busy getting her house ready for Brad's party that evening. She was a tiny thing, coming up to Haven's shoulders. Her brown eyes twinkled with merriment, and she moved like she was being chased by firecrackers. But Haven also sensed that simmering just beneath her surface was a fire that could be lit by any passion, be it social injustice or the love she so obviously shared with Brad. Haven looked forward to getting to know her better. Jake told Haven about the party and wanted her to go with him, and she earlier agreed, convincing herself she would need the respite after an emotional afternoon. She laughed when Brad whispered in her ear later that he was going along with the surprise end of it because he didn't want to hurt Beth's feelings.

"What are ya'll whispering about?" Beth asked as she walked up behind them. Brad shot up with a start.

"Nothing, honey. I was just filling her in on some of Jake's dirty little secrets in case she was thinking about him the wrong way. That's all, sugar. Did I tell you how much I love you?"

Beth laughed as he snuggled into her neck, determined to kiss away her questions in order to avoid her discovering his knowledge of the party. "You are, by far, the weirdest man on the planet. Haven, has he always been this weird?"

Haven threw up her hands, but Jake answered for her. "Yes, Beth, he has always been this weird. It was determined when he was very young through some extensive genetic and biological testing that his weirdness is the result of a gene mutation and nothing that can be inherited. So my future nieces and nephews need not fear. Brad's weirdness is all his own."

The boys continued their bantering until Mrs. Baker blew a very loud whistle by placing her fingers in her mouth. Everyone immediately returned to their eating, and all the while Mrs. Baker flew back and forth between the kitchen and the table, filling their plates with homemade chicken and dumplings, corn pudding, slap-out biscuits, and a slice of lemon pie for dessert. Haven didn't remember eating and was surprised when Mrs. Baker collected her empty plate from in front of her. She was even more surprised to see how quickly the time passed. She hugged Jake's mama much easier on her way out of the door, thanking her for all she'd done for her and especially for her father while he was alive. Mrs. Baker merely clucked in response, tucking a tendril of Haven's hair behind her ears and pulling her roughly against her soft bosom.

"Lean on the Lord, Haven. He'll take care of things for you," she said softly into her ear.

The door closed behind Haven, and the world seemed to grow smaller. It was as if she had fallen asleep, as though it wasn't really her walking toward Jake's truck, going through the motions that would lead her back to the funeral home. But the dream kept going. No one woke her up. And suddenly, she was sitting alone with her father, sitting beside him, working up the courage to finally say her good-byes. She grasped the cold hand that had rarely touched her with affection, and yet she finally felt the love that flowed from a heart no longer beating.

CHAPTER 11

Jake was waiting for Haven outside the viewing room, knowing the reception area was already full. He had been helping his mom and her United Methodist women friends to set up the tables and flip out tablecloths as big as bedspreads. He gave his mother a nod towards the door and scooted up the stairs to sit on the folding chair outside Harry's viewing room. When Haven opened the door a few minutes later, he took her hand and led her toward the stairs. Neither said a word. None were necessary as they made their way down the back steps of the building. The door at the bottom opened into a kitchen, which would allow them to enter the meeting room through a silent swinging door. It would give Haven enough time to adjust to the crowd. Somehow he knew she'd be overwhelmed.

Jake thought the only way you knew this was a funeral and not a wedding was the fact that there were so many different people. If it were a wedding, they'd all look the same. But Harry Stunham brought them all together. Elderly men with skinny ties and white short-sleeved button-downs stood in groups next to the money crowd as if waiting for a train. None really intermingled, except the noticeable politicians and, of course, Bobby Downer. Jake and Haven entered behind a U-shaped table that was laden with brunch-style food like little quiches, cut-up fruit in a carved-out water-melon, and chicken salad sandwiches and beautiful hand-cut flower arrangements scattered among the silver serving dishes. Mrs. Marshall Cole stood behind a separate table to serve the white grape/ginger ale punch from her great-grandmother's silver bowl into delicate crystal glasses. She knew how many she brought and never left with fewer. She had stood in that very spot for every funeral and wedding since 1963, when her mother passed the ladle to her. It never occurred to anyone not to invite her.

Jake knew the few girls who had actually made it out of Sugar Bend and married someone not of the South would come back for their hometown weddings with an almost theme park atmosphere. And Sugar Bend would proudly host the Ferragamo-clad imports with hay-bale seating at the barbecue rehearsal dinner and fill the dry-docked canoes with ice and beer. They were proud to take them on a tour of the state antebellum homes, never seeing the giggles behind manicured hands or hearing the exaggerated drawls their guests would mimic in the bathrooms. It never occurred to them to question why you had to hire a barbecue caterer out of Atlanta when Uncle Poke's slow-smoked was good enough for you growing up.

But Jake knew funerals were different. Here, you were burying your own.

At once, the crowd noticed the two of them standing off to the side. They descended on Haven like flies on butter. People came by, shaking hands, introduced as Representative so and so, House Speaker so and so, Mayor what's his name like passing landscape. How did all these people have so many stories to tell of her father, and she not even know their names?

Haven didn't see a familiar face until the door opened and Clancy Rutledge walked in with a rotund lady, black and majestic, wearing a flowing purple chiffon gown and matching oversized hat. She was waving a flowered fan like palm branches. Haven started toward them as she could see Bobby Downer out of the corner of her eye. She wanted to be the first to greet them.

But the mayor beat her to the door. Haven held her breath, ready to let it loose if her guests were not welcomed.

She was shocked when he threw his arms around Clancy. "Mr. Rutledge, I'm so glad to see you looking so good. It's been too long. How's Doug doing?" She could feel Jake squeeze her shoulder as if to say, "Give it a minute."

Clancy easily returned his embrace, his starched shirt crinkling as the two separated and pumped hands.

"Doug be doing fine, Mr. Mayor. Thank you for asking. He's still practicing law over there in Atlanta, but makes it home now and then. I'll be sure to tell him you asked."

"You better tell him to call me next time he's in town. I don't think I've seen him since our reunion coupla years ago. Now, Mrs. Rutledge, forgive me for being so rude. Don't you look pretty?"

The conversation continued for a little while, others joining in to welcome the Rutledge family. "Now, how about that?" Jake whispered in her ear, leading her around the group gathered by the Rutledges. She placed a hand on Clancy's back. When he turned, he pulled her close and said, "I guess this town done fooled both of us, huh?"

Haven could only nod as Jake pulled her away to greet the other guests. She did her duty, masking her grief under a cloak of calmness that she didn't feel. And ever-present beside her was Jake, whispering names in her ear, touching her gently on her back when he felt her sway on her feet. When Bobby called everyone into the celebration room, Jake guided her down another aisle so that she could slip in the front and take her seat. Unasked, he sat next to her in the pew during the memorial service, laughing softly as Harry's supervisor at the mill recalled the one day Harry called in sick to work in thirty years, and he promptly called an ambulance to his house because he knew it must be serious. Imagine Harry's surprise when his midnight game of poker had lasted into the morning hours, only to be disrupted by the paramedics charging through the door. And all the while, Haven discovered a father she never knew.

After several more eulogies and a slightly off-key rendering of "The Old Rugged Cross" by Allison Temple, most recently named the county junior miss, who was honing her musical talents at funerals and weddings, Bobby Downer asked the congregation if anyone else would like to speak. Clancy Rutledge slowly got to his feet, waited a moment to get his balance, and then began walking. He was sitting toward the back, so it took a while to walk up the aisle. He seemed unaware of the eyes that followed him curiously. He climbed the few steps by pushing down on each knee and shuffled to the podium. He adjusted the microphone down to his height and began to speak.

"It is right and good to be in the house of the Lord," he began, taking out a handkerchief to wipe his brow. He wore chocolate-colored polyester slacks. His short-sleeved shirt was opened at the neck, where his skin folded in layers through the opening. But his eyes swept the crowd as if daring them to interrupt his time. His wife let out a quiet "Amen," and several looked back, more out of curiosity than annoyance. Ad-libbing church time was as foreign to them as snowfall. Each religious service, be it Methodist or Episcopalian, ran like a corporate meeting. And the preacher would hear about it by the time he got through with lunch if it didn't. They accepted Bobby's solicitation for speakers as polite and on the agenda. Not something you actually did. More than one wondered silently if this would run over their afternoon tee time.

"The Lord giveth, and the Lord taketh away. Praise God for Harry Stunham. Give God the glory for his life. Harry been done worshiped with us out there in the county for many years now—never missed a Sunday. Bet you didn't know that, did ya? Naw, ya wouldn't have 'cause Harry didn't need to do his preachin' in public. But he loved His Lord, and the power of Jesus done called him home. Halleluiah in the name of Jesus!"

Mrs. Rutledge gave a "Preach on!" Several of the other attendees nodded toward Clancy. Others just squirmed in their seat. Before Clancy was through, though, there wasn't a dry eye or an untouched heart in the house. Tee times were long forgotten.

He spoke of Harry's mission work in the poorer parts of the county. How he faithfully brought a week's worth of groceries to a widowed woman named Essie, a woman who, in her eighties, was too crippled by arthritis to get to the grocery store, much less church. Harry would bring her groceries and read from her Bible every Sunday after church. Clancy spoke of the tender way Harry closed her eyes on the one Sunday he walked into her house when he didn't hear the familiar "Alriiiiight" drawn out long and loud to make sure whoever was knocking would hear her. Miss Essie had crossed over to the Promised Land, he told the crowd, waiting on Harry to come read her Bible. Her fingers were resting on 1 John 4:23, "And this is His command: to believe in the name of his Son, Jesus Christ, and to love one another as he commanded us."

"Listen here to Clancy, folks. Harry done right by the Lord. He did love others as commanded by our Lord Jesus Christ. He mighn't have professed it with his mouth in a public way, but he sure showed it. If you're here today for Harry, then do as he did. Find your joy, folks. It's there you'll find your Jesus. And Jesus is the way, the truth and the light. No one shall come unto the Father except through Him. And Jesus, you good folks should know, is good and simple love," he ended and slowly walked away from the podium.

Marianne Baker gave a loud, "Amen!" as he passed her pew and then put her hand up to her mouth with a smile, embarrassed. As if receiving permission, the rest of the congregation stood and clapped while Clancy took his seat.

Bobby nodded to Haven, giving her the cue to exit the service. She trembled as she walked from the altar to the rear of the committing room. It was as if it were some reverse bridal procession because everyone remained standing. She began to feel the whispers of those behind gloved hands and knew despite the uplifting service, there were judgmental eyes on her back. She knew they loved Harry. What she didn't know was their love for her. All she could feel were words like, "Look at that girl. I wonder what is wrong with a child that makes her own mama leave her?" or "Isn't she a strange one? Never hardly talks to anyone." The whispers floated around her like heat vapors from asphalt after a summer rain. She squared her shoulders and held her head high and proud, determined to show how she shook the red clay from her shoes the minute she left Sugar Bend, Alabama.

Jake, however, heard different whispers. He heard, "Look at that beautiful girl. Bless her sweet heart. How her daddy loved her." Or, "Haven sure has grown up. I know Harry was so proud of her. He always talked about how good she was doing." He wondered why her jaw was clenched so tightly, her mouth stretched too thin to be a natural smile. He chalked it up to the stress of dealing with losing a parent and gently guided her up the aisle.

The sky had cleared as they stood outside the funeral home and said their good-byes to the many she had not been able to speak to at the reception that preceded the service. Clancy gave her a wave as he helped his elderly wife into the antiquated black Ford pickup truck in need of a paint job and a new bumper. There was to be no graveside burial. Harry was adamant about that. In fact, his body wasn't even present at the memorial service. "I'll be danged if I'll have people gawking about me, saying how good I look when I know good and well I look like one of them mannequins Harland keeps down at Fred's. No, sirree. You listen to me, girl. You dress me up to see my Maker and then send that Downer boy and his workers to put me in my hole. I don't want you to see that—you hear?" There was no arguing with Harry when he was in one of those moods. Besides, Haven couldn't believe they were actually having that conversation. It never occurred to her how limited her time would be with Harry. Fate had tricked her again and took from her when she vowed to always be the one leaving.

"Haven, you ready to go?" Jake asked quietly, interrupting Haven's thoughts. When he saw her haggard expression, he took her by her elbow and led her to his truck before she had time to protest. The drive back across the river was quiet, as if nature was quietly returning respects to a man that had done the same in kind. Even the bridge construction was at rest, and Haven unconsciously rolled down her window to take in the river smell as they sped over the rickety bridge.

As they crunched into the driveway, stray branches of pine scraping against the hood, she turned to Jake. "Listen, Jake, I appreciate all you've done for me the past few days. But I think I need to be alone for a few hours. I need to go through Harry's things, get his papers organized. I've got to leave first thing in the morning and have a lot to do."

"What can I help you with?" Jake asked, almost anxiously, not wanting her to be alone.

"Not one thing. Really, I'm fine. Plus, I really do just want to be alone. I feel Harry more when I'm at this place, and I'd like to spend some time with him. But listen, give me directions to Brad and Beth's, and I'll be sure to see you there later," she assured him, taking a pen and a discarded envelope from her beaded black bag. Jake felt guilty about the fact he noticed her skirt had slipped up her knee, revealing the creamy skin littered with freckles.

"Besides, you've got to remember, I'm used to taking care of myself."

"I'll bet you can," Jake replied under his breath, not intending on saying the words loud enough for her to hear.

"I swear you men are all alike. You know what I mean!" Haven said in mock offense, but with a smile. "I just meant I could take care of myself."

Jake looked at her incredulously. "Oh, come on. Give me a break. You expect me to believe you don't have a steady boyfriend over there in Georgia getting down on bended knee each night begging you to marry him?"

"Never had one ask me to marry him, no. I usually never let it get past the first few dates."

"Why's that?"

"I don't really know. Something about commitment and me just don't go together. I work a lot, and being in real estate, there can be some pretty crazy hours. Most guys aren't willing to let their woman have a strong career. So I just keep it to a few dates, few kisses now and then, and nobody gets hurt," she said, not wanting to admit the real reason, that the thought of getting close to anyone gave him too much power. It allowed him to leave her. And she knew he would eventually. Harry just proved that.

"Sounds kind of lonely, doesn't it?"

"Maybe to some people. But remember, there's a big difference between being alone and being lonely. Most people aren't comfortable with themselves, but it's all I've ever known."

Jake didn't think Haven realized that as she talked, her tone carried a tinge of regret. She was looking over her right shoulder, out the open window of the truck. He was embarrassed to note a few dirt smudges on the windshield in front of her that he neglected to get off when he washed it the other day. And he still hadn't fixed that crack that snaked down to the wiper blades and gave the glass an electric look when hit directly by the sunlight. He could only imagine the type of men that dated Haven now. They certainly owned more than three pair of Carhartt jeans, and their undershirts weren't permanently stained under the arms and around the neckline with sweat.

Raking his fingers through his hair and loosening his tie, Jake cleared his throat. "I find your not having guys lined down the street hard to believe, but to be honest with you, I can certainly relate. I always let Brad be the heartbreaker of the family. Here," he said, reaching for the pen and paper. "Let me write it down; it'll be easier. I'll give you my cell number, too, so you can call me if you run into trouble finding it. Mama is bringing Brad by around seven, after he fixes some made-up problem in her bathroom. I think Beth has him insisting she come to dinner, but he will have to bring her because we took the spark plugs out of her car so it wouldn't start."

"I thought there was no surprise at this point. Brad told me earlier he knew all about it," Haven said.

Jake chuckled. "Yeah, everyone knows that but Beth and Mama. And don't let her find out. I saw enough of her temper back when she was settling DeJesus' file to know I'd never want to be on the receiving end of one of her tongue-lashings. I know she looks innocent, but man does she ever come alive when provoked. She's like one of those bears you see on TV. The ones that look so cute that kind of wander along minding their own business. But then they rear up on their hind legs, and the world's a different place. No, sirree, not me. If she does find out about Brad spoiling the surprise, I'll be the first one out the door."

Haven placed her hand over Jake's with her other on the door. "I don't know how to thank you for today. You've been such a good friend. I don't know if I'd have made it without your being there."

Jake held her hand a little longer, even when she turned to leave. He brought her fingers to his lips, giving them a gentle kiss. "You don't have to be in this alone, Haven. I'm not going anywhere."

Unnerved, Haven slipped off her heels before stepping out of the truck, not wanting to navigate the gravel drive in anything but bare feet. She gave a slight wave to Jake, refusing to dwell too long on his words. *He's just a nice guy. Always has been,* she reminded herself and took the few concrete steps in one hop to let herself into the screen door.

There's nothing more solemn than returning to the home of a dead person. The walls almost sag in grief as they discover themselves orphans, breathing in an almost audible sigh, as the air carries a different smell. Haven felt as though she'd walked into a stranger's home. She sat on the oval woven rug that ran the expanse of the room and gave a full account of Harry's death to the surroundings that comforted him all those years alone with her and then, well, just alone. Folding her long legs underneath her Indian style, she struck a familiar Yoga pose that she and Lila practiced on an irregular schedule. And she talked.

"Harry sure did love this place. I have a feeling he loved it more than anything, certainly more than my mother if he was unwilling to leave it for her. I wonder sometimes if he loved it more than me. Don't you think the proper thing would have been to move to town, grow up with other kids, and not feel like such a freak?" Haven asked rhetorically, shaking her head as she realized she never could have left the river either.

"I guess that's the one thing me and Harry had in common, our love for that old muddy river. I can't imagine growing up not having it to rock me to sleep every night. Do you think Harry was happy?" Falling into the silence, Haven recalled the good times with Harry, particularly things like when he taught her to swim or how to pick out poison ivy from the harmless undergrowth. They'd go for long walks through the woods as soon as Haven could toddle after him. The first time she left the house unannounced, he knew he'd better get her familiar with her surroundings quickly because no four walls would ever keep her contained.

"See those leaves there, girl? There, at the bottom of that oak? Count the leaves and tell me how many it has on each shoot."

"One, two, three," only Haven's th's were more f's, and it sounded like "free."

"That's right, three. Stay away from those three-leafed plants around these trees. It'll make your skin red, and you'll have to take a bath in oatmeal."

Haven remembered how exciting that sounded, and that's exactly what happened when Haven didn't heed Harry's instructions and walked right through a patch of poison ivy. She knew exactly what she was doing. She was just too stubborn to accept something at face value without proving it for herself. And Harry did as he promised. She bathed every night in oatmeal to help the itching and covered her arms and legs with calamine lotion until it felt like it was part of her bloodstream. Thinking back, she remembered blowing her nose and it coming out pink, although she's sure that couldn't have happened.

"I remember one walk down by the water," Haven continued, never thinking it strange that she sat in the middle of an empty room talking to herself. "Harry had started back toward the house, but I was straggling along, picking wild flowers along the way. I saw a black snake in the bushes by our path. It was going real slow. I remember how distended it was in the middle. I walked right up to the snake and picked it up around its head—just like I'd seen Harry do to a garden snake one time. I ran to catch up to Harry and show him.

"I'll never forget the look on his face when he saw me carrying that water moccasin. It was distended because it had just eaten a mouse, and that was probably the only thing that saved me. That, and the fact that I held it so tightly at the base of its head that it couldn't reach around to bite me. Harry told me, 'All right, girl. That's real good. Let's walk over here to the shed and see if we can find it somewhere to sleep. Whatever you do, don't let go 'cause we wanna keep it. It'll run away if you loosen up.' I just laughed and skipped beside him. I wasn't about to let it go 'cause I was gonna make it my pet. Gracie is the only animal we've ever been able to keep around here 'cause she's just so darn jealous."

Haven smiled when she remembered walking to the shed and Harry reminding her not to let go of the snake. He slipped his hand under hers and then told her to back up once he had a grip. Before she knew it, Harry had taken a hand axe and cut its head off. She cried the rest of the afternoon and didn't stop until Harry got out a National Geographic book on snakes and read to her about the danger of water moccasins and showed her a picture. It wasn't until she compared the picture in the book to the snakeskin Harry had cleaned that she accepted the danger of her situation.

"But remember," she continued. "I was only five."

Haven didn't realize how long she sat on the floor of Harry's living room until she noticed the shadows spreading over the patchwork sofa. It was then she looked around the den. She began to see things that were always there, but she never really noticed. The hand-stitched, framed cloth over the front door that read, "As for me and my house, we will serve the Lord." She saw the worn Bible on the aluminum TV stand next to Harry's recliner, opened and waiting. She saw a cross hanging by the back door and one on the counter holding down a stack of papers. Were these things here all along? She never gave them any notice. They were just part of the house—kind of like the curtains. But now she knew they had meaning and was saddened not to know what that meaning was.

She glanced at her watch to see most of the afternoon gone, and she'd not done one thing she'd intended to do that afternoon. She got to her feet and hurried down the narrow hall to Harry's bedroom. After changing into a pair of blue jean capris and a white T-shirt, she began going through the armoire.

After years of filing cost analyses for first-time home buyers, dealing with the mounds of paperwork involved in obtaining FHA approval, and the many settlement statements that she returned to clients at year-end to help with their taxes, it did not take Haven long to get her father's things in order. The bank statements were balanced, and Haven was glad Harry had insisted on her last trip home that he add her name to his account, thereby eliminating any need to provide a death certificate or probated will in order to disburse funds. There was more than enough money to keep the homestead up until Haven decided to sell or keep it as a second home for herself. At the time, however, she couldn't imagine ever returning without Harry here, but couldn't imagine selling it, either. There was also an original and a copy of Harry's will, a very simple document, given his limited resources. It would be an easy matter to probate, and given that he left everything to Haven, she could then decide what to do with his belongings. She did find an aged shoebox labeled "HAVEN" in black marker written in Harry's hasty scrawl and held together with duct tape. She assumed it was old report cards and such and placed it by her suitcase to go through back home in Georgia.

As the kitchen cuckoo clock chimed seven times, Haven hurried to take a shower, wondering what you wore to a party filled with people you hadn't seen in five years. People she rarely saw even when passing them every day. She cursed herself for being so late. It wasn't in her personality to agree to a certain time and not show up fifteen minutes early. She pulled a baby blue Donna Karan sundress from the closet and slid it over her head. She kept her makeup simple, a brush of mascara and some lip-gloss. She dusted herself with powder, cursing her freckles as she did every day since puberty. Thinking the night air might have cooled with the earlier shower, she grabbed a white shrug from her suitcase and slid her size nine feet into Jimmy Choo white sandals adorned with gold and silver jewels. She never thought about the names she now wore around her shoulders and on her feet. She didn't reflect on the chasm between her cutoffs and the designer clothes she was wearing tonight. She just learned over the years to wear what Lila told her, initially buying designer knock-offs, moving to consignment boutiques until she could eventually purchase a $500 dress for herself and not think twice about it. It reminded her of wrapping paper, easily discarded. She quickly moved her wallet and keys from her beaded black bag to a more casual straw shoulder bag and ran out of the door.

Within fifteen minutes, she was pulling into Brad and Beth's empty driveway, assuming it was okay to park in view, given the fact that Brad should have arrived forty-five minutes earlier. Everyone was to have parked down the street to hide the cars. She was relieved when Brad himself opened the door wearing a paper crown someone brought from the local Burger King. An old '80s hit was blaring from an unseen stereo, and she recognized only a few people. She pulled on her ponytail as he led her into the den, introducing her to people whose names she tried to recognize along the way.

It was an eclectic group, an almost descriptive melting pot. Several African-American couples sat in chairs around the buffet table. One man looked at what Haven assumed was his date and said, "Don't make me go all Johnnie Cochran on you," to which she replied, "Daniel, Johnnie Cochran is dead." He was silent for a moment before he replied in mock seriousness, "Yeah, well, we still tight."

Haven recognized a girl from high school that took a sip from a cup offered to her by a young Mexican man. She masked her wonderment at the changes the few years made in Sugar Bend. The hometown she knew segregated itself comfortably by race and economics. And only during athletic events or charity work did they cross-pollinate. She was pleased to see the Bakers did not choose their friends based on color, age, or any other predisposition category.

A conversation from a showing a few years ago came to mind as she recalled a young military couple in which the husband had just returned from Iraq. He was telling her about his tour of duty, emphasizing a particularly harrowing night during which the company endured constant ground attacks. He credited his partner, Manuel Chardonnay, with keeping his sanity as well as his equipment in check with his good humor.

"That's an unusual name," Haven had commented. "Was he Hispanic, French?"

The soldier thought for a moment. "You know, I don't think I ever really asked. It was more important to me that he knew how to shoot a gun. Luckily, whatever ethnicity he was, we both went home the next month," the soldier replied. It seemed as though the Bakers allowed that same racial anonymity to be applied in their house, and Haven longed for the nonconformity of Lila and Mark.

Brad interrupted her reminiscing by excusing himself in the den after getting her a glass of wine. She walked toward the kitchen while searching for Jake, but instead found herself face to face with Roxanne Williams.

CHAPTER 12

"Well, Haven, welcome home. I'm so sorry to hear about your father," Roxanne drawled slowly, her cat-green eyes giving Haven a dismissive once-over while feigning sympathy. "Jake was just telling me the other day about you gracing us little peons with your presence this weekend. Such a shame it took your daddy dying to bring you home."

Roxanne brushed by Haven without giving her a chance to reply, leaving Haven to glance at her black tank top plunging low to reveal deep cleavage. The sexy top was in stark contrast to the loose, rather unflattering sweater, and Haven thought it odd the way she kept tugging it around her. Roxanne was never shy about showing off her breasts since they made their premature appearance in the sixth grade, but tonight she didn't seem quite as eager. She was rocked by the savagery of her words. It had been a long time since Haven had experienced such viciousness.

"Thanks for your condolences," Haven muttered under her breath, fighting against that age-old sense of insecurity that assaulted her whenever she was faced with the more popular crowd growing up. She suddenly felt awkward and alone and wondered for a minute if she should just let herself quietly out the front door. Suddenly, a croaky laugh coming from the swinging door to her right got her attention. She excused herself around a young couple leaning against the stacked stone fireplace and gently opened the door to the kitchen. Sitting at the table, oblivious to the party going on around them, was a young Mexican boy and Ruth.

"You have to lean your head down and drink it upside down, Ruth," the young boy Haven guessed to be DeJesus said while demonstrating just that. Ruth just rocked back in delight, clapping her hands and pulling on her old royal blue Windbreaker, hiccupping painfully every few seconds.

"Hey, Haven. Did you know that most lipstick contains fish scales?" she said, hiccupping, when she caught Haven out of the corner of her eye. It was as if no time had passed—like they were still in the halls of Sugar Bend High School, kindred spirits not quite sure where they fit. Although her hair showed a few strands of gray and there were more than a few laugh lines around her eyes, she had not changed a bit.

"No, Ruth, I didn't know that," Haven replied, pulling up a chair. "Who's your friend?" she asked, after the young boy gave a shout of disgust to her fish scale trivia fact.

"This is Jesus. He's my friend. He's trying to get rid of my hiccups," she said, letting out a stream of hiccups in response.

The boy just smiled in Ruth's direction. "It's really DeJesus, but Ruth has a hard time saying that, so she just calls me Jesus," the young man replied. He had the curliest black hair with a texture that gave Haven the impression of some African-American heritage. His skin was coffee-colored, and he had large brown eyes that looked like the muddy river waters after a good rain. He looked about eight.

"It's nice to meet you, DeJesus. Jake told me a lot about you. Ruth and I've been friends a long time, haven't we, Ruth?"

"Yeah, but you left. You left without saying good-bye. Why'd you do that?" She pulled her jacket tight around her, leaning forward with both hands pressed between her knees as if fighting off a chill.

Haven felt chagrined for a moment. She could hear the laughter from the next room, and the kitchen door continually opened and shut with people congregating out on what Haven assumed was the back patio. The kitchen was simple with black-and-white-tiled floor and white cabinets against a stucco wall. She thought for a moment before she replied.

Why did she leave so quickly? Was life in Sugar Bend really all that bad? But Haven knew the answer. It wasn't that it was bad. It just wasn't any good—at least for Haven. She was like a wound-up kite in her childhood, longing to fly the skies at the first good wind. And when she left, it was as if Harry unrolled and then let go of the line. She knew she needed to forge a new life without any constraints of the child she thought she was. Or more importantly, the child she thought others perceived her to be. Somehow, she could never imagine becoming an adult alongside those who never really embraced her as a child. Not that she ever gave them the opportunity. It was strange how confusing her thoughts had become over the weekend. The town she felt so strongly against suddenly seemed to cloak her in such a warm sense of familiarity that she was finding it difficult to hang onto her childhood perceptions. Little did she know that Harry didn't let go of the line; he just tied it around a river rock. And while she'd have enough slack to pursue her purpose, she would always remain tethered to the river.

"I don't know, Ruth. I guess I just had things I had to do. But I can promise you this: You were one of the few that I missed a whole bunch. Do you think you could forgive me?" She leaned forward and forced Ruth's hand into her own.

"Sure thing," hiccup. "I'm not mad. I know you wanted to leave. Knew for a long time." Hiccup.

"How'd you know?" Haven asked incredulously. DeJesus just watched in silence as the two talked, giggling occasionally when Ruth would hiccup.

"Just knew, that's all. You had to go find you some friends. I like friends. They're good for your heart. But I'm sure glad you came back. You see Roxanne?"

Haven nodded in agreement, leaning back in her chair while taking a sip of her wine. "Yeah, but she didn't have much to say."

"Yeah, she still don't like me much either. But that's okay. Somebody needs to be her friend if it's not going to be me. Mr. Mike is a bad person."

"Who's Mr. Mike?"

"That's her husband. He hits her lots, and nobody does nothing about it. Did you know that more than 10,000 birds die each year from smashing into windows?"

Haven didn't have time to answer because the door swung open, and Beth blew in, carrying a stack of plastic cups and napkins. Haven jumped up and took a load from her hands.

"Thanks, Haven. The garbage is just behind that door, in the pantry. My goodness, this is more work than I would have thought. I didn't realize everybody that I invited was going to come along with their mamas and cousins." And with that, she was gone after retrieving a steaming dish of cheese dip that left a lingering smell of sausage and peppers in her wake.

While Haven was in the pantry, she noticed a jar of peanut butter. She searched through the drawers until she found a spoon. "Here, Ruth. Try this. Ruby used to give me peanut butter whenever I had the hiccups, and it would take them right away."

Ruth clapped her hands again in delight, opening and closing her jacket. "Oooh! I like Ruby. She gives me chocolate kisses. Did you know a peanut is a legume and not a nut?" She snatched the spoon away from Haven and ate the entire helping in one bite.

"Thanks," she said, which came out more like, "Twnks" due to her full mouth, and laughed out loud when she realized the hiccups were gone.

"Dude, that's amazing!" DeJesus exclaimed. "How'd you do that?"

He jumped up and grabbed Ruth's hand before Haven had time to reply. The two bounded out of the back door as if their name had been called in the playground game of red rover, leaving Haven alone in the kitchen.

Taking another sip of wine, she contemplated again whether to give the Bakers her good wishes and excuse herself. She felt beat down by the day, both physically and emotionally, and was confident anyone would understand her need to call it an early night. She stood from the table, making her way outside, as that seemed to be the direction Beth headed when she left the kitchen earlier. Opening the door, she carefully let herself out onto the small deck.

She immediately met up with a group of three women, one of whom she recognized as Lindsey Melton, who was a year younger than Haven in high school.

"Haven! I heard you were in town. I'm so sorry about your daddy, honey. Come here and let me introduce you to my friends," she said sincerely. Lindsey was slightly over-weight, with kinky brown hair that curled up in the spring humidity like dried-up worms on a driveway. But her smile was genuine, and Haven remembered her kindness from school.

"This is Marsha and Marilyn. They grew up a county over, but moved to the big city when they married some of the imports that paper mill brings in from time to time."

Haven smiled a shy hello and stood awkwardly with the group.

"We were just discussing the wonders of stay-at-home motherhood. Do you have children?" Marsha asked, continuing when Haven shook her head and said she wasn't married. "Well, lucky you. I'm just kidding, sort of." She looked to be about Haven's age with the rounded hips childbirth often provided. "I called a friend the other day, and when I didn't get her, I just left her a voicemail. She called me back laughing that it was the longest voicemail she'd ever heard. I told her that's 'cause it was the only adult voice I had heard in a week!"

Haven laughed with the others. "How old is your baby?"

"Ten weeks, thank God. But can someone please inform him that is the time he is supposed to sleep through the night? I'm so tired of smelling like sour milk and having to make love with my nursing bra on that it's driving me crazy."

"You're already having sex?" Marilyn asked incredulously.

"You mean you're not? You know the doctor releases you after six weeks," Marsha admonished. Haven remained mute, not really having anything to offer, but was intrigued by the conversation. It was like watching a foreign film with subtitles.

"I know that, and you know that. But your Travis doesn't have to know that," Marilyn replied. "I told my doctor I was having serious postpartum depression, and he needed to back me up if Jason ever asked him when we could have sex. Not that he would ever grace the door of my gynecologist. I feel lucky he even made it to the birth considering it was opening weekend of bow season."

"Hey, did you guys see Roxanne? I guess she's back to wearing sweaters to cover up those bruises," Lindsey said, taking a step closer to the group and lowering her voice. Haven glanced around and saw Roxanne through the window into the den, standing by herself. She had her arms wrapped around her waist, looking around the room as if surprised to find herself alone. She walked over to a group of men that included her husband and was ignored as if she'd never walked up.

Marilyn dropped her voice in response. "No doubt. Jason told me that Mike doesn't hide that he hits her. He has even been bragging about how he knocks her around. Claims it establishes him as the man of the house, how he doesn't have to 'put up with all the lip you other men have to listen to from your women.' " She held her fingers up like quotation marks when adopting a deep, masculine voice.

It would have been so easy to join into the gossip; there would have been some justice in desecrating a reputation just as those had talked about her those years ago. She wondered how someone as popular as Roxanne could end up alone in the corner during a party. But somehow she couldn't find it in her heart to do anything more than take another sip of wine and glance about the yard.

Tiring of the topic, Lindsey made some remark about continually tearing up the kitchen sink because the plumber was that hot young Mexican that the Baker boys often used in their contracting business. "My husband didn't pick up on it until the third bill came in, so he called my hand. The phone guy is some old fart in his sixties, and the yard guy is actually a lesbian, which is disappointing because I originally found her quite attractive. So I'm still trying to find some repairman that will give me my 'Desperate Housewives' moment."

The three ladies laughed easily together, and Haven joined in, noticing for the first time the back of Jake standing with his weight on one hip at the bottom of the steps leading into the small yard. She started to excuse herself to go toward him when he shifted slightly, and she could make out a small blonde laughing easily to something he said.

Lindsey noticed her glance. "Oh, girl. Brigitte's had her sights on Jake Baker since he took her out last year. I think he was the first guy who never tried to get in her pants, and she's been trying to change his mind ever since. Looks like tonight she might get lucky."

Haven gave a forced smile and returned her attention to the girls. "I've always imagined being a stay-at-home mom is about the hardest job there could be. Am I right?" she asked, hoping to divert their attention from Jake Baker's sex life. And she couldn't have chosen a more appropriate subject. Haven easily slipped away while the women bemoaned the fact there was no end to their days, no sick hours or vacation time. And everyone seemed to think that not getting up and going to a real job gave her so much more opportunity to volunteer for church, PTA, and on and on.

"But we're supposed to have our breast pump going full blast while running on the treadmill with the baby monitor turned up in case Shelby wakes up in the rare fifteen minutes she sleeps," Haven heard Lindsey remark.

Haven made her way through the house, pausing a few times to talk to people she recognized from the funeral. She spoke briefly to Mason Turner, a guy from her eleventh-grade English class that spent the majority of the year with his nose in a circle drawn by the teacher on the chalkboard because he was constantly rearranging the desks every time she would go to the bathroom. He wrote in her high school annual, "Here's to all our good times. Well, the ones I had by myself at night when I thought about you. Let's get drunk and party sometime this summer." He still had a face that looked like it climbed off a wall in the post office. He was one of two signatures in the book and only because he swiped it when she was throwing her food away in the cafeteria. The other one was Ruth, whose childish handwriting scrawled, "Love to me, Ruth." Haven stopped to give Brad and Beth a quick hug and to thank them for thinking of her.

"Did you not see Jake?" Beth asked quietly. "You can't leave without saying hello. Let me go see if I can find him." She began to walk away.

Haven pulled back on her hand. "No, no, really that's okay. I'll give him a call next week," Haven assured her quickly. Brad merely raised an eyebrow at her quick response. "He was talking to someone outside, and I hated to disturb them. Plus, I really need to get back because I've got to get home early tomorrow. I never did get a chance to speak to your mom, Brad. I hope you'll let her know how much I appreciate her kindness."

Brad took her by the arm before Beth could continue her protestations because he noticed how Haven's eyes drooped with fatigue and emotional expense. He led her to the front door after giving Beth another reassurance that she was okay. They both stopped, and Brad gave her a gentle hug.

"Be good to yourself, Haven. Give yourself a chance to let someone be good to you. I have a feeling you deserve it," he told her softly.

Haven was at a loss for words and let herself out of the door instead. She was relieved to know her car was not blocked in from those revelers who were even later than she in arriving. It wasn't long before she found herself driving down the winding roads beside the river.

She caught a glimpse of white as Gracie raced around the house, the headlights from Haven's BMW giving her a scare. She made her way easily in the dark, opening the door to let herself once more into her childhood home. Although it had not felt like home to her in quite some time, it held the memories of a childhood she would now have to put to rest. It was a rather touching moment, as she knew when she entered it would likely be the last time she would ever sleep here. It wasn't that she didn't love the river. It wasn't even that she didn't hold some regard for Sugar Bend. But she had grown so much in the five years since she left. The person she left behind was almost unrecognizable to her, and she knew beyond a shadow of a doubt that the woman she had become could never make a home here. But she decided to pay homage to her one more time.

Haven grabbed an old threadbare robe from the back of her daddy's bathroom door, inhaling the scent of his cologne that smelled like pine trees. She carried it with her out of the door and made her way blindly down the stone path leading to the water.

The gently flowing water created wrinkles in the moonlight cast upon its shoulders. It reminded Haven of when Harry taught her to make shadows like animals with her hands using a flashlight and a white sheet. The water shimmered like a satin sheet, wanting and needing to envelop her—to rock her to sleep once again with its lullabies. The river was a chameleon, ever-changing to accommodate the needs of those who sought it, but always there. While some would slingshot themselves across her shoulders on Jet Skis, others would row along her shoreline in makeshift canoes or paddleboats. Didn't matter to the river. She just aimed to please.

Haven shed her clothes, leaving her dress in a crumpled heap on the wooden dock, and eased herself into the water. It was shockingly cold, causing Haven to draw in her breath. But she quickly acclimated, giving quick, sure strokes until she found herself in the center of its womb. And there she rocked on her back, allowing the moonlight to bathe her in its milky lather. And she felt herself slowly heal, allowing the cleansing of the water to once again give her permission to leave if that's what she needed to do to make herself happy. She didn't know if leaving would, but she was almost sure that staying would not.

So she swam slowly back to shore, rolling onto her back occasionally and spitting out the water like a whale's spout.

She pulled onto the dock and covered tightly in her daddy's robe, almost like a blanket of security around her shoulders. She did not cry again, but instead fought hard against the familiar feeling of loneliness in her heart. "Alone, not lonely," she reminded herself as she so often did through the years. "At least no one is left to leave me." And she walked up from the dock with that assurance.

She walked toward the house, the silence interrupted by an incessant knocking on the other side. She heard Jake shouting, "Haven!" as she hurried through the screen door and across the den. He stumbled into the room, surprised when she opened the door as he was in mid-knock, and almost landed on his face.

"Jake, what is it? You almost scared me to death!"

"Scared you? You scared me, girl! Why didn't you answer the door?" He looked both frazzled and relieved, sitting on the arm of the recliner while he caught his surprised breath.

"I was taking a dip in the river, if you must know. What are you doing here? I thought you had a big night planned with Brigitte?" she asked in a slightly huffed tone, surprising herself with its intensity.

"Brigitte? You've got to be kidding me. I had told her before all this happened with your dad that I MIGHT meet up with them down at the Cellar for a drink, but I can assure you, that's all I meant to do."

"You don't owe me any explanation, Jake," Haven replied, still maintaining a huffy tone. "What is wrong with you," she admonished herself under her breath as she reached around Jake to close the door.

Jake stood and took Haven by the shoulders. "I'm not giving you an explanation, Haven. I'm just stating the facts. I couldn't believe you left Brad's without even saying hey. I decided to stop by here on my way home to make sure you're okay. Mind if I stay awhile?" Jake grinned at Haven, and her heart just melted. She noticed for the first time a slight scar along his jaw line. She ached to run her finger across it.

"Yes, I do, actually," she said in mocked offense, taking his arms from hers and turning away quickly before he could see how easily he affected her.

"Tough. I don't want to go home, and you could use some company."

"Oh, I could?" She turned back toward him.

"You could. Now scoot. You smell like the river. Matter of fact, you smell just like you always did as a little girl. Go clean yourself up. I'm going to find some George Jones that Harry was always playing on his record player and fix us both a stiff drink. Go on now, get. Go do something with that hair," Jake said, turning Haven's shoulders around and giving her a swat on her behind. Haven dropped her jaw and gave Jake a dirty look over her shoulder, but half jogged to the bathroom just the same.

Jake found the dusty album collection on the shelf below the ten-inch television and selected the perfect choice right on the top. After several tries, he finally placed the needle in the primary groove and closed his eyes to inhale the twangy tunes. Turning from the stereo, he slowly made his way to the kitchen, stopping once to place his bent arm to his stomach and his other outstretched as if leading a beautiful lady in an imaginary dance. But he knew from the heat building up in him from the last few days that he desperately needed that dance to become a reality very soon.

CHAPTER 13

J ake was carrying two whiskey tumblers into the den with
a bag of chips and a jar of cheese sauce he had heated
in the microwave when Haven returned wearing the same
white T-shirt and jeans from earlier. Her hair was hanging
to her shoulders, still damp from her attempt to towel dry
it after her quick shower. Her feet were bare with perfectly
polished toes painted red in stark contrast to the white of her
skin. Jake took it all in with one glance, then quickly turned
away before allowing the flesh side of him to override his
good sense.

"You know, you ought to wear your hair down more
often. Maybe run a brush through it every now and then,"
Jake teased while handing her the whiskey. He had built a
fire, although the temperature did not call for one. But he
opened some windows, and the gentle breeze off the river
balanced out any small heat the flames provided.

"Hey, that's not the first time you have criticized my hair.
What is it with you and hair?" she asked, sitting beside him
on the floor with her back against the couch and taking a few
chips from the bag. The light from the fire flickered across
her face, illuminating her freckles in a primitive dance along
her cheekbones.

"If I tell you something, do you promise not to tell anyone?" he asked innocently. His face took on that of a small boy; scared to reveal something in the event the person had his fingers crossed behind his back.

"I promise. Scout's honor," Haven replied, holding up two fingers and solemnly nodding her head.

"Scouts are for boys, and you, my dear, are most assuredly not a boy. But I will trust you anyway," he paused for effect. "I have a thing for women's hair."

"You what?" Haven exclaimed, almost choking on her drink of whiskey.

"It's true. I have always been in love with women's hair. If I thought I could make a living out of it in Sugar Bend, I would play with women's hair all day. I used to spend hours brushing my mom's hair growing up. I loved it when Brad spent the night away from home 'cause I could play with her hair until my heart was content. That's the one secret my mom swears she'll take to her grave."

Haven turned to look carefully into his eyes and found he was telling the truth. And her heart melted like butter on toast to think of this epitome of masculinity sitting for hours brushing his mother's hair. She looked away before he could see the tears starting in her eyes.

"Now, before you say anything, I promise I do not have some sort of fetish about hair. There definitely has to be more to the package to turn me on, so don't go thinking there's some Freudian explanation for my hobby. I just love running my fingers through it. It's always so soft and smells so good. You're laughing at me," Jake cried, trailing off his conversation as he noticed Haven giggling behind her hand.

"No, no, I promise. It's just wild to think about, that's all," Haven laughed out loud.

"I'll teach you to laugh at me," Jake cried, lunging toward Haven and knocking her to the ground. He immediately proceeded to tickle her over the thin fabric of her

T-shirt. Haven kicked and howled and rolled free, with tears streaming down her face in laughter. Jake rolled onto his back with his head turned toward her.

"Let me feel your hair, Haven," he said.

She got up quietly and walked back to the bathroom. She returned carrying a brush and sat again on the floor in front of the couch, while Jake sat on the cushions behind her, placing one knee on either side of her shoulders.

The first touch was scorching, as Haven knew it would be. Although not completely inexperienced, Haven was not familiar with the heat true passion could ignite. She never had anyone tell her the consequences of sex without commitment or love. No one shared with her that every time a man touches you, he takes a piece of you with him. And so one night several years ago, she gave her virginity to a guy she barely knew who was as inexperienced as she. She remembered thinking, *That's it?,* because the encounter left her empty and more than a little sore. And a piece of her walked out of the door with him. But being with Jake was like finding that piece of her again.

And Jake brushed.

First he ran the brush through her blonde hair. The light from the fire created highlights that he hadn't noticed in the daylight hours. Her hair popped with electricity once it was tangle-free, and Jake enjoyed watching it follow the brush as if it were a magnet. Then he placed the brush on the couch, and beginning at the base of her head, he ran both hands up the sides, gently pressing with the heels of his hands while massaging with his fingers. And he talked softly in Haven's ear.

They talked about everything and nothing. Jake shared with Haven what it was like growing up without a father. Haven was surprised to hear that he shared many of her same insecurities, but elected to not allow other people to label him by things he had no control over. He knew it was easier for a boy to be accepted in the small-town South. Athletics leveled the playing field for the guys. But he let her know he knew of her loneliness growing up, but felt powerless to do anything about it.

"I used to watch you and Brad play cup ball when you guys stayed here during the summer. I'd sit up in that big oak and try not to laugh when Brad would get mad at you for beating him," Haven said.

"Why didn't you ever come over to play with us? Brad could have used all the help he could get."

"That's a good question. I don't know. I guess I was just too shy. I remember when he threw your basketball in the river that time you never let him score. It's funny the things you remember," she replied. "You remember that time your cousin Debbie came to visit? She had that life-sized Crissy doll. The kind you could pull her hair out to be long or roll it back in for short hair. I remember wanting that doll so bad. I grabbed it before she realized she left it outside, but Harry made me bring it back. He switched my hide good for that one."

"Yeah, I do remember that. She was so spoiled. I think she's on her fourth or fifth marriage by now. You deserved that doll more than she did."

"Funny how that doll ended up in the tree beside my bedroom. Wonder how it got there?" she asked rhetorically.

Haven could feel Jake laugh behind her. "Funny things happen down here on the river, Haven."

"Shoulda known," was all she returned.

Jake smiled with her as he changed the subject. He told her about Roxanne and the life she led now. How her husband caused her to miscarry when he pushed her down a flight of stairs, forcing an emergency D and C. How she really didn't have any friends.

"Why would she stay with someone like that?" Haven asked through the fog of relaxation that was creeping up her body.

Jake continued running his fingers along her scalp. "Some people think it's more important to keep up appearances because if they accepted help, they'd have to admit there was a problem and everything wasn't perfect. I've offered to take care of things many times, but she just looks at me like I sprouted wings and offered to fly her to the moon. Some people just don't trust others to love them for who they are."

Haven considered those words in her heart. They fell into a comfortable silence then, Jake continuing to run his fingers through Haven's hair. He knew it would be like this. Even as a child, he entertained notions of brushing Haven's hair. His fingers subconsciously made their way down to her neck, gently skimming along its surface. He wasn't sure she realized that she turned her cheek into his hand as he moved down to her shoulders.

The innocent brushings coupled with the tension was getting to her. Haven reached up and took his hand. "Let me feel you, Jake," she whispered, taking his hand and placing it to her. It was as natural as breathing. Jake's voice was low in his throat as his thumb moved over her skin. He was fascinated with her softness, worrying that his calloused hands would tarnish the perfection of her pale skin. Both of their breathing increased, and beads of sweat popped out on his brow that had nothing to do with the temperature of the room. Neither realized that Jake had left the couch and joined her on the floor.

The couple moved together as if in a slow dance, George Jones crooning about how he stopped loving her today. Jake was just beginning to love Haven. He was fascinated by every inch of her, studying her closely as a new set of plans.

When they finally came together, it was as if they'd never been created as two separate individuals.

After loving her, he pulled her to him, touched by the fact he could feel her tears wetting his shoulders.

"You okay, Haven?" he asked gently, brushing her hair off her face without allowing her to look up, feeling her smile into his chest.

"That was just so amazing, Jake. I never knew it could be so beautiful," she spoke, her voice muffled.

"That's because you've obviously never made love. It's more than just about our bodies, Haven. Have you ever read the book of Solomon?"

Haven rolled over, propped up on one elbow and shook her head, "What is that, some new book? You trying to tell me you've read something I haven't?"

He smiled. "No, Smarty Britches. It's in the Bible. I don't have mine handy right now, but next time I'll have to read you a few passages. Right now, you'll just have to trust me to show you."

He spent the rest of the night doing just that. He scooped her up into his strong arms and carried her into her childhood bed, where he proceeded to show her how to love with more than just their bodies. Finally, they lay in each other's arms, allowing sleep to overcome them. Haven slept with no dreams for the first time in her memory.

In the pre-dawn hours, Jake eased out of bed, careful to not disturb Haven and dressed in the dark. Pausing at the doorway, he stood watching Haven sleep. She was lying on her back in the moonlight, the pale, faded colors of her childhood comforter pulled up to her waist, practically undisturbed. The stress lines of the weekend were gone, her complexion smooth. Jake leaned his head against the doorframe, his heart constricting with an overwhelming sense of protectiveness. She looked at peace and completely...vulnerable.

The thought stopped Jake in his tracks. He squeezed his eyes to the thought.

I didn't take advantage of her, Lord, trying to convince himself. *I'll make this right. When I get back, we'll figure out how to make this right,* he prayed silently.

Haven awoke later than usual, the sun well on its way up the skyline. She smiled warmly to herself, stretching her arms out to encourage blood flow to her lifeless limbs. It was then she noticed that she was alone in her bed. She rolled over to face a note lying on the pillow next to her.

Haven,

Sorry for not being here when you woke up, but you looked se beautiful. I hope you don't find it too creepy, but I watched you sleep while I drank my coffee. There's monkey bread in the refrigerator. It's Mrs. McClendon's so you know it's good!

Anyway, I had some business at Mom's and needed to run over a few things with Brad. I thought I could drop by around lunch, and we'd figure out where to go from here. Can't wait!

Love,
Jake

She bolted upright in bed, her heart hammering against her rib cage as if she'd run a mile sprint in under five minutes. LOVE! DO TOGETHER! Those were words Haven swore she'd never face again, now that she'd outlived or outlasted the few who said those words to her in the past. She couldn't stay with Jake, could she? That would mean living in Sugar Bend, acclimating herself to a town where she had spent her childhood purposefully in the peripheral boundaries, content to wander down its motherless streets. She had finally left all of that behind her. Why in the world would she go back?

But thoughts of Jake interrupted her rationale. She could still feel his fingers on her arms, caressing her back while he held her close. He told her he would never leave. Could she believe that? She dared to lift the corner to glimpse at what could be, and the tight fist that lived in her core began to loosen. Maybe she could stay; maybe it was time to finally belong to someone else and learn to share her life with someone that she loved. Maybe he really wouldn't leave.

But an internal fury raised its head from the throne of her consciousness, slammed the lid on all her maybes and scoffed at her naiveté.

"Are you kidding? Jake deserves someone of his own kind. You saw how loved he and his family are in this town. You saw how well he fit in. He deserves to be with someone like Brigitte. Someone who had a normal life growing up and knows how to be a wife and a mother. He was even quoting you the Bible! You've never really been to church! Get out of here quickly, before he comes back; you know it will be better for everyone. You know he'll leave you in the end because you could never make him happy. You couldn't even make your own mother happy!" the fury screamed at her, feasting on age-old insecurities and perceptions.

Haven fought back by instinct. "Why can't I have this? Why for once can't I love someone who obviously wants to love me?"

But the fury held strong, enraged that Haven would even consider fighting back. "In love with you? What a joke! If he was in love with you, do you think he would have slept with you? He wanted one thing and one thing only. And he got it! Plus, you saw how close he is with his family. You saw how easy they were with each other. There's no way you could fit in with that!" And with that, Haven was defeated.

Before she gave it too much thought, she jumped out of bed with determination and a quick glance at the clock. She grabbed a pen and paper and wrote a short note to Jake, thanking him again for all the care he had shown her the past few days, how she would have loved to stay, but she just had too much to do back home and how she would be in touch. She didn't leave her number and had enough foresight to tear the page that held her personal information out of Harry's phone book. She pulled on a sweat suit and matching Windbreaker, grabbed her keys and sunglasses off the bathroom counter, and slid her feet into the raggedy black flip-flops she found on the floor of her closet. She didn't even bother locking the door.

Haven threw her clothes in her car, not bothering to place them neatly in the matching Louis Vuitton luggage and merely hauling that in the trunk, forgetting the shoebox with her name on it, left on the kitchen counter. She slammed the trunk closed, jumped over the door to the convertible and fishtailed out of the driveway. She knew she had to leave this life behind her once and for all. What she didn't realize was that the life growing inside her would lead her so quickly back.

CHAPTER 14

Haven stayed at the door for a few seconds, allowing herself one more glance at her beautiful daughter sleeping. She was all but swallowed up by the massive purple comforter that wrapped around her like a cloud, her black hair fanned across the pillows that encased her body. Ever since Lauren moved to her big girl bed last year, she insisted on pillows surrounding her body, allowing her perfect access to their softness no matter what direction she turned. It reminded Haven of when she was in her last months of pregnancy with Lauren, how no position was comfortable. She would surround herself with the highest count of down-filled body-sized pillows in the hopes something would support her just enough to give her that good night's sleep she so desperately needed.

But she never had a mother to tell her that she would never have another good night's sleep again. She would spend every half-hour during that first year bent low over the bassinet to make sure her daughter was breathing, to make sure Lauren would not leave her. No mother told her that she would struggle to breathe through every newscast that reported on missing children or how the movie *Steel Magnolias* would be banned from her DVD collection. The closest maternal conversation she had during her pregnancy was when Lila tried to convince her that a glass of wine was actually good for the baby, regardless of what those silly classes tell you down at the hospital.

"Come on, Haven. Just one glass. I'll bet Jesus' mama got her a few sips riding that donkey across the desert," Lila implored, sitting cross-legged on the Persian rug that ran the expanse of the hardwood pines of her living room. She and Haven were waiting on the good-looking delivery guy to bring their Thai dinner. Lila tried to convince her that not only was wine good for her, but all that silly heartburn was really just in her head. Haven merely belched in response.

"Jesus' mama was only thirteen years old when she gave birth, Lila. Even I know that. I hardly think that would qualify her for an RUI," Haven replied.

"What's an RUI?"

"Riding under the influence," Haven said and joined her in laughter as the doorbell rang with their food.

Haven walked back to her bedroom after carefully shutting Lauren's door, remembering the way Lila picked her takeout more on a little-known ingredient called good-looking than on the actual meal itself. God love her, she gained ten pounds eating Sticky Fingers ribs and potato salad before the blond pre-med student that was home for the summer got himself fired for having sex with a divorcee out in the county. It wasn't so much the sex that got him fired as it was the free barbecue they ate after. Having learned this, Lila declared she would never buy from that chain again. How dare they believe stolen food was more criminal than his choosing some county trash to fool around with when he knew good and well he could have roamed those greasy hands all over her anytime he chose. Theft could be forgiven. Ignorance — never.

What would I have done without Lila? Haven thought to herself.

The year following her father's death was compounded when Haven visited a general physician who congratulated her on her pregnancy rather than writing her a prescription to cure the virus that stormed up her stomach all day each day for several weeks running. She kept the news to herself, walking around in some sort of haze for the next month, most days just trying to pretend it wasn't happening. She would feel a familiar cramp and run to the bathroom to relieve herself, wiping deep in the expectation of seeing that familiar brownish stain that came on the first day of her cycle. Each time she would even remotely feel a cramp, she would close her eyes in gratitude, wondering how she was going to fulfill all the promises she had made to a God she had rarely spoken to until recently. But it never came. And she would drop her head into her hands and wonder what in the world she was going to do.

As usual, it was Lila that provided her with the answer. Unfortunately for Haven, she wasn't one of those women who sailed through pregnancy like it was a simple cruise around the islands. No, she spent many visits over any random, cracked toilet, no matter what time of day. She could describe the inside contents of the most obscure bowls, having christened most of them with very little warning. Just a roll of her stomach and a slight increase in saliva, and out would come the morning's raisin bran or lunch's turkey sandwich. She wanted to strangle the person who termed this condition "morning sickness." What a joke!

It was Lila who came by work early one morning, intent on finding a tube of "Carrot Cake" lipstick before her meeting at the Chamber of Commerce. What she found was a bedraggled Haven, clutching the floor of the employee bathroom, the back door wide open, as that was as far as she had made it before losing what Haven hoped was a bland enough bowl of oatmeal.

After calling in her regrets to the Chamber president, Lila mopped Haven's face, walked her into her office, shut her door and turned angrily, "You want to let me in on the father?"

Haven gave Lila the full story, not sparing any details. Lila realized fairly quickly that arguing with Haven about telling Jake about the baby was falling on deaf ears. There were no words to persuade her it was the right thing to do.

"He didn't ask for this, Lila. He's got his life in Sugar Bend. And I've got my life here. I can raise this baby by myself. I can learn how to be a mama."

So Lila gave Haven all the love and attention she would have given her own children had God allowed her to bear them. It was Lila who brewed ginger tea, spiking it with a shot of whiskey when Haven wasn't looking. It was Lila who discreetly told everyone in the office of Haven's decision to have the baby alone and how any of them would be fired if they offered an opinion that was anything other than, "That's great, Haven. Let us know what we can do."

"And I don't want to hear no talk about sin and hell and anything remotely related to that," she said, looking pointedly at Mandy, who was already preparing her sermon in her head. Mandy was determined to bring every person she encountered to Jesus, even if she had to strong-arm them to do it. It made for a slow real estate career.

Lila attended the childbirth classes, learned how to breathe during labor, and passed out twice while practicing at home. She would walk around her home on weekends with a pillow under her blouse in order to gain more knowledge of how it felt to be pregnant. She only succeeded in vowing not to be a fat girl.

And during her entire pregnancy, Haven only endured a few glances down on her ring finger and raised eyebrows when noticing it bare. But then as her pregnancy advanced, people no longer seemed to notice, probably because even if she were married, it would take a ring the size of a hubcap to fit over her swollen fingers.

But it was during those rare quiet moments when Lauren would be still, the sounds of the world muffled by the gentle flow of her mother's womb, that Haven would stroke her stomach and wonder. Is this how my mother felt when she carried me? Did she smile when I would get hiccups and jump like a cricket in her belly? Did she worry about what kind of mother she would be? Did she feel unworthy of the unconditional love her baby would have for her like I do? Haven would pretend that she did. It was inconceivable, given the love she already felt for her baby, that any mother could feel any other way.

And five months, three days, and twenty-three and a half minutes after Lila found her in the bathroom, working right up until her water broke on the way to a Realtor caravan, Haven held Lila's hand as Lauren Elizabeth Stunham entered the world after four good pushes.

"Haven, I have to admit that's one of the fastest first-time deliveries I've seen in quite some time," Dr. Kim Williams spoke from between her legs as she scooped Lauren up in a towel. "Come here, Lila-daddy, and cut the chord."

Lila clapped her hands in delight and skipped to the end of the birthing bed. "Wow, Haven. From this angle, if I were a man, I'd get my feelings hurt by looking at how big that thing got. You'd never be able to convince me there's a man alive that you'd be able to feel during sex again," she said, waving the scissors in the air.

Haven lay back on the pillow and managed a weak smile while Dr. Williams guided Lila's hands above the tourniquet on the baby's chord. "Let's not make her bleed before we have to," she gently chided Lila.

Haven watched tears course down her best friend's cheeks as she cut Lauren's chord. She reached out and grabbed Haven's hand.

"She's so beautiful. I can't believe you did this. I can't believe any woman can do this. What a miracle. Every cliché anyone ever said about this experience is running through my head right now, but none of it seems adequate. I am so proud of you," she choked out, bending down to give Haven a kiss, paying no mind to the black mascara running rivers down her cheeks.

As Dr. Williams continued to work on Haven, the nurses placed a cleaned-up Lauren into Haven's arms.

"She weighs eight pounds, six ounces and is nineteen and a half inches long," the nurse announced to the room, turning from the bed as she wrote it on the card.

"Hey, little girl," Haven whispered softly to Lauren's fuzzy black head while Lila leaned over both of them. "It's just us against the world. Think we'll make it?"

"I know you will," Lila replied with confidence, knowing she wouldn't allow anything less.

Haven gave up on reading. She closed her book, turned to place it on her nightstand, which already had three more books going, with two more on the chair in the corner, and turned off the light. Like running, reading had always provided an escape from reality. From the moment she began to read chapter books in the second grade, Haven often would retreat to unknown worlds through the pages of her books, worlds she had never visited but hoped to one day. Worlds in which mamas and daddies had dinner with their children, mamas braided hair before school or waited on the porch until children returned. Books where everyone lived happily ever after. She loved visiting those places. It was what she loved most about selling real estate. She worked hard to help families find the homes for their happily-ever-afters.

She scooted to the middle of her queen bed, never knowing what it would be like to share it with someone else. She lay on her right side with her hands folded under her cheek. She sent a prayer up to the same God that Harry kept so private. She asked Him for forgiveness for keeping Lauren a secret from those that would have loved her. She also asked Him for the courage to face the news Dr. Jones would give her in the morning and guidance on what to do next. After waiting too long for an answer, she finally surrendered to sleep.

CHAPTER 15

Haven knew the message wasn't good from the look on his face. She had arrived early, anxious to hear the results of whether she was a candidate for Lauren's kidney transplant. Tired of passing the time with outdated Hollywood rags and elevator music, she began counting the dots on the tile ceiling, praying for this God of mild acquaintance to show her how to save her child. All kinds of promises floated up, ranging from adopting underprivileged children in India to a return to steady worship services. Parents of dying children will only admit to themselves the extent they'd be willing to go to heal their children.

On more than one occasion, Haven had driven past an unassuming house out on the highway with a hand-painted sign extending out of the front yard. It read "Sister Lee, Faith Healer, Palm Reader." Each time, she hit her blinker, her subconscious driving her actions to take whatever means necessary to save her child. But traffic would always multiply, congestion forcing her to try again another day. Somewhere in her heart, she knew people like that made their money off people like her. Desperate. Frustrated. Controlling. But that didn't stop her from considering it. Haven's thoughts were interrupted when the door opened. Desperation once again entered the room with the look on Larry's face.

169

"I'm sorry, Haven," Larry said, putting his files down on his desk and folding her into his arms. It was a casual embrace, but familiar. "We can't use your kidney for Lauren. We've got to look at other options."

The test had consisted of a simple blood test followed by a general evaluation of Haven's physical well-being. Although the analysis took most of the afternoon, she had to wait until Larry could clear his calendar to go over the results. But she would have waited longer if it meant she could control the disease that was intent on destroying her daughter.

"What's wrong? I know we're the same blood type. I've never been sick a day in my life. What could possibly be the problem?" She asked, shocked, convinced that all the testing was merely a formality.

"It seems you've developed a slight heart murmur. Or maybe you've had it all along, and we happened to catch it this time."

"What's a heart murmur?"

"A quite common occurrence, actually. As the blood flows through the heart chambers, it makes a swooshing sound. If one of the chambers doesn't close completely, the blood flows back into it slightly, creating an offbeat sound. It creates a potential for infection. It's nothing to be alarmed about. I'll schedule you for an echocardiogram just to be sure. It will probably mean just taking an antibiotic before you get your teeth cleaned or if you ever need any type of surgery," he answered.

Haven chewed the side of her mouth for a moment, arms crossed over her chest. "Well, if it's so common, why should that stop me from giving Lauren my kidney?"

"Live transplants are highly regulated, Haven. If there's any glitch in a person's health, we're not allowed by law or medical oath to perform any elective operation on that person. That's why there's such a waiting list for organ donations. It's just so hard to get someone approved."

An emotion flowed through Haven as if her blood was on fire—rage. "No bureaucrat is going to tell me what I can and can't do for my child! I don't care if I'm wearing a pacemaker! If my kidney is what she needs, why can't she get it?" She yelled in frustration, pacing around the room, arms clenched by her side. Her mouth took on the feel of a sailor on leave with rarely used curse words spewing forth. She returned to Larry and folded naturally into his arms, grabbing his jacket with her fists. Why did God hate her so much? What had she ever done to deserve this?

For a minute, she just held onto the white jacket and allowed Larry's strong arms to hold her. Her heartbeat returned to normal as the reality of the situation sank into her mind. Finally, with a strong squeeze in return, she pushed off his chest and wiped her eyes.

"Well, we both knew this was a possibility. What's our next step? Because let me tell you something, Larry," she turned and looked him square in the eye with hard determination. "I refuse to let that baby die. It's not even a remote possibility. She will not leave me. I don't know how, but I just know there's no way I'd let her go. No way that can be right. I just can't," Haven couldn't finish her sentence, tears of frustration coursing down her face as she silently cursed the fate that brought her baby to this moment.

Larry held her again, giving her a moment to collect herself before he continued. Outside the door, he could hear footsteps of those working in the hospital. A page announced the need for Dr. Wynne Nelson to attend the ER stat. And outside the window, two birds conversed through the pines about the simplicity of a life that didn't weigh them down with the unnecessary emotions humans obtained when loving children.

Larry guided Haven into one of the two coffee-colored leather, nail-trimmed gentleman's chairs in front of his desk and took the other. "Two options. One I've already begun. I made some calls, emails, and faxes and put Lauren on the priority list for a kidney transplant. Listen to me, Haven. We could get lucky. I have seen miracles beyond my understanding. We could just catch a break. The second option you'll have to handle. If Lauren's father and his family are an option, you've got to contact them to get them tested immediately. If someone is a match, we'll have to get him or her here for an emergency transplant. Our time is limited. We've got to move fast, or else we're looking at other organ failure. I'm not here to scare you, only to be realistic about the facts," Larry said, not unkindly. His face softened.

"Let me let you in on a secret, too. I refuse to lose Lauren or put you or her through any unnecessary pain. I'm in this to the end. And by the end, I mean a healthy toddler on her way to becoming a young lady. Don't ever doubt we can make that happen."

He took Haven's face between his hands, gently stroking her cheekbones with his thumbs. It was a bold gesture, one he had never ventured before. But the two had shared more intense moments and conversations than most marriages. Haven didn't find it inappropriate. She turned her head and leaned into his embrace, feeling safe for a moment.

She pulled back from him, smiling into his eyes as he brushed the tears from her face with his thumbs. "Thanks for being here, Larry. It seems I'm always saying that, doesn't it? I don't know what I'd do without you."

"I do. Exactly what you've done so well all along. I'm just blessed to be a part of both your and Lauren's lives in whatever role that is. You know how much I care about you, Haven. I won't try to hide that from you. Never been good at deceit, anyway. We'll get through this—all of us."

Larry walked around his desk and sat in his office chair with the harbor waters glistening over his right shoulder. Haven knew Larry was a sailor and kept his sailboat docked a few blocks away. He had promised to take them on a sunset cruise around the bay when things settled down. Haven retrieved her well-worn notebook from her briefcase and began taking notes about the necessary paperwork for the transplant list, which included insurance forms. The procedure itself would wipe out Haven's savings account, even with insurance paying 80 percent. He advised her to prepare any questions she may be asked by Jake's family in order to provide the answers they needed. She pushed away the reminder that one of the first questions the family was bound to ask was about Lauren herself, given the fact they knew nothing of her existence. She'd just have to worry about that detail later. It was too minor when compared to saving her baby's life.

"Where's Lauren now?" Larry asked when they were done.

"She's with Lila. I've got a closing at four, and then I have to get some information entered for the MLS book for some new listings I got last week. Mark thankfully took some pictures for me yesterday while we were here getting Lauren's vitals checked."

"You know, part of me wants to tell you to take a break. Let me help you out financially so you can concentrate on Lauren and not kill yourself in the process. But the more I've gotten to know you this past year, the more I know you'd go insane doing that.

"So I tell you what. I'm through here at the hospital. How about I run by Lila's and pick up Lauren, and we'll meet you at my house, where I'll fix you girls some dinner? Lila, too. How does that sound?" It felt strange to be this nervous. It was the first time he'd asked her to his house. They had occasionally shared a meal at the hospital after some of Lauren's dialysis treatments, but never to his home. It was impetuous and completely out of character.

"Normally, my first reaction is absolutely not. Especially given what you've done for us already. But here's a compromise. Lila is actually meeting me at the office at five with Lauren after they go have their toes jerked. That's what Lila calls pedicures. I'll certainly invite Lila, but Lauren and I will be more than happy to come to dinner," she said with more enthusiasm than she felt. Actually, all she wanted to do was go home and start the day over, insisting on a different result from her compatibility test. And she wondered if by accepting this offer, she was giving the impression she was ready to take that innocent embrace a little further. And then she wondered if she really cared.

Haven pressed the enter button on her computer just as the door down the hall jingled open and a joyful, but tired voice yelled out, "Mommy?"

"In the back room, honey," Haven called, anxious to see how the afternoon had affected her daughter. Lately, any kind of simple activity seemed to exhaust Lauren, so much that Haven almost refused Lila's kind invitation for a girly afternoon. As Lauren entered the room, Haven was relieved to see some color on her cheeks and a smile that could replace the fires of hell with sunshine. She gathered her in her arms and breathed in the scent of her hair, a mix of baby shampoo and fingernail polish, a result of an afternoon with Aunt Lila. She met Lila's eyes over Lauren's dark head and communicated the bad news with no words at all.

This nonverbal universal language among women was fascinating to Haven, having only experienced it in the years since leaving home. She never lay side by side with other elementary girls on pallets pulled in front of a static-filtered TV long after the stations signed off. She never lathered another teenage girl's skin with a mixture of baby oil and iodine, inviting the numbing rays of summer to shimmy through a sky that still held onto its ozone layer. There were no giggles over long-distance dedications that Casey Kasem produced each Saturday afternoon. Those early conversations were the ones grown women would mold into volumes of words spoken without sound. Luckily for Haven, it was a quick learning curve, childbirth allowing her to catch up. No matter what age or circumstance, race or creed, women speak loudly through minimal eye contact and communicate all the wonders, loves, losses, mistakes, and joys that are theirs and theirs alone.

"I'm so sorry," Lila mouthed back, tears threatening to spill down her cheeks. She called out that she had to run to the little girls' room for a minute and hurried out the door to hide her emotions.

"Are you okay, baby girl? You didn't do too much, did you?" Haven asked anxiously, pulling her back and checking her face more intently. She did notice some fatigue lines around her dark eyes, but that was it.

"No," she answered.

"No ma'am?" Haven reminded her.

"No ma'am," Lauren replied with a smile.

"Did you have fun?" Lauren nodded her head. "Did you get your toes painted?"

"Yes ma'am. See?" Lauren wiggled ten French-manicured fingers and leaned back on her heels to show her toes through her sandals. Although it was late September, it was still warm enough for sandals and dresses like the pale pink one that Lauren wore today.

"We sure did have a great day, and that little girl was an absolute doll. After her nap with Sir Gally, we got up and took ourselves to the mall and had a ball. Didn't we, sissy girl?" Lila asked boisterously as she returned to the room, determined to hide her dismay at Haven's news.

"Well, I've got a surprise for you, too, Lauren. Dr. Jones has invited us to his house for dinner, and I told him we would go. He wants Aunt Lila to come, too. What do you think?" Haven asked.

"SURE!" Lauren exclaimed.

"What do you say, Aunt Lila?"

Lila shook her head. "Not me tonight, sugar girls. Aunt Lila is going to dinner with a congressman because she wants to find out if the saying about men with big feet is really true," Lila said with a lascivious grin.

"What do they say?" Lauren asked innocently.

Before Lila could answer, Haven spoke loudly, "Never mind, sweet girl. Let's go to the little girls' room, get your clothes changed, and freshen up so we can head on over there and not be late. Go give Aunt Lila a hug and tell her thank you."

Haven's breath caught in her throat as she watched the two people she loved most in this world grab each other in adoration. Lila held on a little longer than usual, prompting Lauren to wiggle away laughing. But Haven knew Lila was reluctant to let her go, hating the world that picked on innocent babies like Lauren. Straightening, she gave Haven a questioning look.

"Dr. Jones, huh? Well, that ought to be fun, girls," she said, giving Haven a suggestive look.

"It's just dinner, Lila. Don't get excited. Come on, Lauren. Let's go potty and hit the road," she said, shaking her head at Lila with false humor on her face while her heart continued to break inside. She looked deep into Lila's eyes and knew she felt the same.

CHAPTER 16

It was a rather short drive through town before Haven pulled into the gated subdivision called Pinnacle Point, gave her name to the security guard posted at the entrance, and made her way through. The immaculate streets were lined with native oaks that blanketed the sky as if trying to touch the tips of each one's fingers. Several children raced toward her on the sidewalk to her left riding scooters and skateboards while a family of five rode matching bikes with safety helmets. It was as if the uniformed guard at the gate only allowed happiness and good news to drive through in fancy convertibles and foreign SUVs.

Haven looked in her rearview mirror at Lauren in her sky blue halter top that tied behind her neck and matching skort just above the knobby knees of a three-year-old. She smiled when she caught Lauren's eyes, and then redirected her attention to the road signs. Finding the correct road, she turned carefully to the right, keeping a wayward kickball in sight as a young boy of about seven waited for her to pass. The houses were almost identical, although some were brick and some stucco. There was an almost Tuscan flair to the homes, typical of these newer subdivisions.

Haven knew that property seldom came on the market in this area. The ones that did sold in the millions. She also knew that Larry had bought his forty-five-hundred-square-foot home on a cul-de-sac about six months ago from a friend that was relocating out of the country. She also knew from other Realtors that he bought the house after his divorce was final. She didn't want to hear any more, but unfortunately, the seller's Realtor was a colleague, and even worse, knew of Haven's connection to Dr. Jones. She wanted her to put in a good word for a date.

"Tell me about Dr. Jones, Haven. I can't get him to say a word about his personal life, and he never mentions having a wife. He's Lauren's doctor, isn't he?" Samantha Mathers was relatively attractive, but carried herself with the erect spine of an upper-class childhood. She had that New England look of pale skin and a sharp nose. Haven thought she would be perfect for Larry and was closer to his age than she.

"What am I thinking?" Haven spoke to herself. "What difference does it make how she compares to me?" Haven just politely changed the subject. And quite frankly was annoyed by the tacky way Samantha included Lauren's condition into her efforts to win the affections of Dr. Jones.

Haven found the house easily and pulled in behind Larry's Mercedes. She retrieved the bottle of wine from the back seat and helped Lauren from the car. Smoothing her hair behind her ears and adjusting the waist on her skirt, she and Lauren made their way to the arched doorway and rang the bell. She heard a voice from the back yell, "Haven, if that's you, come on around back!"

The back yard almost took Haven's breath away. It was a beautifully sculpted English garden with boxed hedges lining the walkway like green walls. She almost expected an overweight queen to pop out and say, "Off with her head!" The hedges widened into a common area with a pebble path around the pool. The pool, however, had a lagoon feel, as the walls were natural stone, and the slide looked more like a waterfall cascading through a rock mountain. She saw Larry at the back corner working over a grill in full concentration and walked over.

"Hey, Dr. Larry!" Lauren beamed enthusiastically.

"Hey, yourself, pretty girl. I'm so glad you decided to be my date for the evening. I hope you like corn on the cob because I'm cooking it right here on the grill for you. Where's Lila?" he asked, kissing Haven on the cheek. Haven liked the casual Dr. Jones the best. He was dressed in neatly pressed khaki shorts and a white button-down with blue stripes nipped into his waist with a brown belt. He wore casual sandals, and his face had a slight sheen of sweat on the brow.

"She went to measure a man's foot," Lauren replied companionably. Larry raised an eyebrow to Haven, who merely raised a hand as if to say, "I'll tell you later."

"I brought wine," Haven said, suddenly uncomfortable with this setting. She didn't know if this was the right step to take, but also knew she needed to take it. What was unclear was if she was here for herself or her daughter. "I'll just think about that later," she said to herself.

The evening progressed beautifully, the fall air providing just enough respite from the long fingers of summer that still reached out like a toddler being taken away from its mother. The leaves in the woods behind Larry's property were bursting with the colors of fall, a rainbow of reds, oranges, and yellows that southerners knew to appreciate because it didn't last long. There was never a true changing of seasons in the South. Mother Nature just merely checked her pulse when things got too oppressive, and the trees put on a blanket of color around their shoulders of green. Larry had given Lauren some freshly cut flowers and asked her to arrange them in a plastic bucket. She was in full concentration, so Larry and Haven talked, mostly about him. The evening was as casual as promised earlier. They lay side by side in matching wrought iron lounge chairs. Haven closed her eyes and pretended everything was okay with the world for just a moment.

It wasn't long before Larry announced that dinner should be ready. The three moved to the redwood picnic table just off from the pool. He knew Lauren couldn't eat protein. Her kidneys would not allow it. They ate together in comfortable silence. Lauren chimed in occasionally with her comments of the day, making the couple laugh when she described Aunt Lila buying "slingshots," as Lauren called bras, at someplace that kept secrets from a lady named Victoria.

"Lila told me about them having lunch in the mall and how Lauren kept staring at two ladies at the table beside them. She said that she told Lauren to quit staring at others, that it wasn't polite. Lauren just thought about that for a second and then said, 'Well, can I look at you but still listen to them?' " Haven said, laughing with Larry.

"That sounds like our girl," he replied, holding his hand up for Lauren to deliver a high-five.

"Of course Lila told her that was perfectly okay, all southern ladies needed to learn the art of discretion."

After cleaning up from dinner, the couple returned to the picnic table while continuing the conversation from earlier. Soon the sun began its slow descent, and Larry caught Haven checking her watch while glancing at Lauren resting comfortably in the third chaise lounge. They were all a little full from the steak for the grown-ups, a vegetable-laden salad for Lauren, and homemade apple pie and ice cream for all. Larry truthfully boasted to making the pie himself, a leftover lesson at the knees of his upstate New York grandmother.

"My father was raised on a farm. It was more of a sustenance farm than the recreational farms around today. My family lived on that land for generations, starting with my great-grandfather, who came over during the Irish potato famine," he recalled wistfully. "I remember my grandfather had a great number of beehives. Thousands of bees were in the hives around the pastures. We all knew to leave them alone and let them do their job."

"What job does a bee have?" Haven asked.

"Bees are a very important part of farming, even today. They provide the cross-pollination needed to keep the fields green with clover for the cattle. I never knew of a real farmer that didn't keep up with his bees. You have to watch the hive, make sure the queen bee is thriving, make sure the worker bees are out foraging the pastures for pollen. And then clean out the hives for honey to make candles, sweetener, lotion, and all sorts of things. You'd be amazed at how important a bee is," Larry said earnestly, taking a sip from his Corona Light bottle. "If I ever got a cut while visiting my grandmother, she would always put honey on it. Did you know germs can't live in honey?"

"No, I guess I didn't know anything about bees, except to get out of their way," Haven replied.

"Don't worry about a little ol' bee, Haven. If you see one flying around you, it's just a worker bee out looking for pollen. Maybe you have on a bright shirt or smell fruity or something. Once it realizes it's buzzing on the wrong flower, it will go away. The only time a bee stings is when it feels threatened. Leave it alone, and it will fly right away."

The two sat in comfortable silence for a few minutes before Larry spoke.

"Haven, can I ask you something?"

"Of course, though I don't think there's much you don't know about me by now," she replied, turning her head toward him.

"Are you content with it being just you and Lauren? I mean, I don't mean to pry, but I've lived in this area all of my adult life, and I've never known a beautiful woman to stay single for long. It makes me wonder if you gave your heart away at some point and that person forgot to give it back."

Haven didn't reply at first. She wanted to choose her words carefully.

"Yes, I'm very comfortable with it being just me and Lauren. I mean, don't get me wrong. I like to have fun as much as the next guy. Lila and I have our regular date nights. Brittany will watch Lauren while we go listen to some good jazz or country music. And I do go out occasionally with other men. I guess I just haven't met anyone that would be willing to take on a single woman and a three-year-old with these health issues. Or maybe I just haven't met anyone I wanted to give that chance." Brittany was the young college girl that babysat Lauren while Haven worked. She was a nursing student and well-versed on how to care for Lauren.

"Well, they're fools, is all I can say. You and Lauren would be a gift to any man."

"I wouldn't be so quick to say that. You haven't seen me in the mornings before my coffee," Haven replied, giving a soft laugh.

I could be so lucky, Larry meant to say out loud. Instead, he placed his hand over Haven's and drew her to her feet.

"Let's walk inside for a minute. I saw you checking your watch, but I want to talk to you in private before you go." Noticing the hesitation that popped up in Haven's eyes, he continued. "Don't worry. As much as I would like to, I'm not going to jump your bones. I just want to talk to you about what to look for in the next few weeks as it relates to Lauren's health. Lauren can watch TV while we talk."

"Oh, okay," Haven replied, relieved, while getting Lauren's attention and holding her hand as the three made their way up the path to the massive deck extending from the back of the home. Haven couldn't help but think about her own deck growing up and the hours she would sit watching the water being gently stirred by the occasional jumping fish. And any thought of home inevitably led to thoughts of Jake. The two were as fused together as the colors of a setting sun over the waterline with never a real point where one began and the other ended. The thought of Jake gave Haven that same feeling she had when she was concentrating on something while driving and suddenly realized several miles had passed that she didn't even remember. She returned her attention to Larry, listened carefully to his advice, and decided not to tell him of her return trip to Sugar Bend that weekend. She was leaving Lauren with Lila to return to the river and to face Jake with the news of her betrayal. She would have to risk losing her daughter in order to save her life.

CHAPTER 17

"You be sure to mind Aunt Lila, you understand, baby girl?" Haven asked Lauren, tucking a stray hair behind her ear. They stood on the stoop in front of Lila's home in the historic district of Sweetgrass. Lila stood by the open door, one arm around Lauren.

"Yes ma'am. See you 'morrow," Lauren replied, tears filling her eyes. The two had never been separated overnight, but Haven couldn't bring Lauren with her to Sugar Bend just yet.

"Don't you worry about a thing. As soon as you leave, this girl and I are heading straight to the video store, renting any movie we want, and eating nothing but ice cream and popcorn until we come see you tomorrow," Lila said reassuringly.

"Okay, okay. I hear you. I'm leaving now. You've got the directions, Lila?"

"I've got the directions to your daddy's house. We'll be there tomorrow with bells on. I've got Larry's phone number, poison control on speed dial, and your novel about what to do in case of an emergency on my bedside table. I've got it, Haven. This ain't my first rodeo," Lila replied, gently pushing Haven toward her car. After a quick kiss to Lauren and a peck on Lila's cheek, Haven acquiesced.

The drive to Sugar Bend took no time, or so it seemed to Haven, who wished it would last forever. She took the time to notice that Clancy's gas station was boarded up. She hoped he was okay, but knew if one person knew where he was going, it was Clancy. It must be nice to have that security in life and whatever waited for you after that.

She entered the city limits, looking for some billboard that would tell her this was all some cruel joke, that Jake was the wonderful man he was, but in Sweetgrass. They had made love under the stars on the beach as man and wife, and both rejoiced after waiting the appropriate three minutes to receive the results of her pregnancy test. But the only billboard looming in front of her was one announcing the fall festivals surrounding the annual Lucky Louis Riverboat Parade.

She had completely forgotten about Louis the Lucky. Haven quickly checked her mental calendar, hoping she had her weekends confused. But no such luck. Sugar Bend, Alabama, celebrated Louis Lemare the first weekend of every October. Lucky Louis was among the French settlers who first came to Alabama in the late eighteenth century hoping to plant grapevines in the impenetrable Alabama red clay. One harsh winter later, all but Louis and his family tucked in their French tails and headed south to Mobile and New Orleans, where they found much more fertile ground in more ways than one. But Louis held on, discovering the benefits of a river that quenched the thirst of those lining the banks with more than its waters. He was soon a very popular bootlegger, running firearms and whiskey up and down the river. He coined the name Sugar Bend in tribute to the limestone bluffs that ran up from the riverbeds capped by the mimosa trees that were grouped together like bridal bouquets in the spring.

In quid pro quo, the town of Sugar Bend celebrated Lucky Louis every fall with a street parade, art in the park, and a riverboat parade at dusk, in which enterprising groups dressed their boats like pirate ships and floated down the river while shooting each other with water launchers. The evening ended with a fireworks display over the bluffs and remained a destination favorite for young families and retirees alike. Haven often watched the riverboat parade alone on her dock, marveling at how little it took for grown men to retreat to adolescence.

Driving down the main highway that dissected the fast food restaurants and gas stations that littered southern highways, Haven began to notice all the traffic she had ignored until now. RVs and pull-alongs crowded the three-lane highway, and Haven braked abruptly as a group of Harley-Davidson motorcycles cut in front of her. French flags flew from businesses, and banners hung below red lights advertising the weekend events. Haven realized that her hopes of getting in and out of Sugar Bend quickly and quietly were next to impossible. Haven had never known the activities to be canceled—not even when the governor of Alabama was shot in the '60s. It would be an insult to the legacy of Lucky Louis. Not to mention hundreds of thousands of dollars the visitors brought in every year that, quite frankly, the town just couldn't do without.

Several years after leaving home, Haven came across a write-up about the festival in an outdated *Southern Style* magazine she found while straightening the real estate office at the close of business. She read about her hometown as if it were a stranger, staring intently at the pictures of the happy celebrations and the people she didn't recognize. It was like looking at the pictures of distant relatives found hidden in the back of the junk drawer in the kitchen, the kind you would stare at long enough in an attempt to disassemble each feature to see any resemblance of yourself and finding none, convincing yourself you were adopted into this family where everyone seemed to have a place but you.

She slowed to a snail's pace as she approached the bridge leading to her father's house after following the detour around the street parade route. "My house," she mentally corrected herself. Haven had not returned since the weekend of Harry's funeral. She had hired a local landscape company to keep the yard up and make sure Gracie was fed, and paid an extra bonus each month to let her know of any necessary home repairs. As she neared the bridge, she noticed a sign indicating the target date of completion for the new bridge was nine months away.

I guess Jake was right. It did take the government forever to get this thing done, she thought. Haven managed the tight turns around the towering pines easily, old habits coming to the forefront, once again reminding her that history had a way of returning to the present. She still wasn't sure or prepared for how she was going to tell Jake about Lauren. It was the urgency of her daughter's health that drove her forward.

Jake finished pouring the food in Gracie's bowl and was returning to the shed when he heard a car rounding the final curve before Harry's house. He stood still when he heard the slam of a car door, watching for whoever would turn the corner.

Haven stopped short when she saw Jake in her father's yard. Seconds passed while emotions gained legs and ran back and forth between them. Jake dropped the feed and was halfway to her before he even realized what he was doing. He stopped, placing his thumbs in the loops of his jeans.

"What are you doing here?" he asked in a rough tone, swallowing the emotion that was threatening to choke the life out of him. Haven was the first and only woman who made him shed tears of longing and anger. He spent months sitting on his boat in front of Harry's house, trying to figure out why she had left. He had tried to find her, only to discover her phone was unlisted and there was nothing in Harry's home to lead him to her. So he merely waited for her to find her way back to him. She never did until now.

"I've got some unfinished business to take care of, Jake. Most of it has to do with you," she answered, approaching him as carefully as a child to a stray dog.

"You don't have any business with me, Haven. Any business we could have had together has long passed its chance. Now, if you'll excuse me, I gotta go," Jake replied, brushing past her as he hurried to his truck. Haven closed her eyes to the scent of him, slightly sweaty with a touch of aftershave. He wore a plain white T-shirt, with one side untucked, and customary Levi's jeans trailing into his brown boots.

"Jake, please wait. Give me a chance to explain," Haven cried, trying to grab him as he passed.

Jake merely shook her off, raising his hand to stop her protestations. "I gave you a chance. I gave you a chance for a long time. All I got was some note telling me you'll keep in touch. What a joke, Haven. Now, like I said, I gotta go." And with that, he opened the door, shut it again hard to punctuate the conversation, and kicked up dirt as he sped down the driveway.

Haven ran her fingers through her hair. *Well, that went well*, she thought. *What now?* She returned to her car, retrieved her suitcase, and went inside the house. She sat for quite some time in the natural light of the windows facing the river, gently rocking in Harry's recliner.

"What's God got against me, Harry?" she asked out loud.

She was surprised when he answered.

"God ain't got nothing against ya, girl. It's just some folks are so darn hardheaded that it takes somethin' big to get their attention. God's usin' this, girl. Don't have nothin' to do with ya 'cept to get yer attention. Make ya lean on Him. Have ya asked Him for help?" Harry asked in his gruff voice, standing in the daylight just outside the door with the river over his shoulders. Haven realized then that she had truly lost her mind if she was now carrying on conversations with her dead father. Or even worse, since he talked back.

"No sir," she continued.

"Well, then, guess ya ain't learned nothin'. Nothin' gonna start getting right till ya ask Him what right is. Take time to listen to Him, girl."

"Time is what I don't have, Harry."

"Well, then, I'd get busy if I were ya. I'll work on it from this end; ya do yer part down here."

"Why are you telling me all this now, Harry? Why didn't you take me to church? Why don't I know this God you talk about now?"

Harry seemed chagrined for a minute. "Should have. I know that now. But I didn't do so bad, did I? Showed ya every day God's glory in that there river—church ain't the only place to find God. All ya gotta do is talk to Him like ya do that river. He'll do the rest accordin' to His will, not yers. And believe me, His will is always better. Ya just gotta let Him take you to it. Now get!" And with that, he was gone. Haven began to pray awkwardly.

Lord, I don't even know how to do this. So, we'll just talk for a minute. First of all, thank you for your blessings. It seems I've spent my whole life running from them. Thank you especially for Lauren. She's a blessing I didn't deserve. But I need your help now. Show me what to do. Help me to know how to get through to Jake so he can see we need him.

She was silent for a moment before mouthing, "Amen." She pushed up from the recliner and strode quickly to the bedroom to change her clothes before she lost her nerve.

God finally talked back. She had a parade to attend.

Jake could not believe the moment he had lost hope in having was already here and gone. There was no definition to the feelings boiling inside his gut at this time. He slammed his fist against the steering wheel while he braked for a flatbed loaded with fresh fruit and vegetables to pull onto the road.

He swore out loud. "Yes, Mama, I cussed. And I'll cuss again. How can this hurt so bad after all this time?" Jake admitted to himself, as much as he hated it, that he could have made love to Haven right there and then as if no time had passed. It was a miracle he had the strength to walk away when all he had prayed for was that moment when he could touch her again. It was the agony of never touching her again that had eaten him up, making his company barely tolerable in the first months after Haven left. Brad had threatened on more than one occasion to buy out his share of Baker Boys.

One particularly explosive argument over what color to paint the garage door on a new spec house resulted in the two swapping punches in their mother's front yard. Brad left in anger, with Jake cursing under his breath while he rubbed his throbbing jaw. His mother came outside with a Ziploc bag of ice and led Jake to her porch swing.

"Baby, we gotta talk. First of all, I heard you cussin', but, well, we'll just have to deal with that later. But right now, I want you to listen to Mama. Don't say a word for a minute and just listen. That's why God gave you two ears, but only one mouth," she said.

"I know you're hurting. God knows I know that hurt. And I know you're mad. You gotta right to be. But you gotta remember what the Lord says, Jake. We can't stay in judgment of other people. There's no sin greater than another. And, Jake, I have preached and preached to you boys about your responsibility to a woman's body. It's about respect, Jake. Her body is a temple to her spirit, and you didn't respect that. If you care about her like I know you do, you never should have touched her unless you were committed to her. That's as much a sin as her running out on you. And your hurting right now is a consequence of that sin. You have one of the hardest heads I've ever known, Jake. You've got a big heart, but an even bigger opinion. And when you get something in your mind, you don't stop to think of the best way to handle something. And, more importantly, you don't give the Lord a chance to show you how to handle it. You just charge into it. You're always cleaning up what you never would have messed up if you'd have just stopped and thought it through.

"You gotta remember, that child is hurting, too. You just don't leave something as precious as you unless you're messed up. We gotta pray for her, Jake, and pray for yourself. I know she'll come back. We gotta know what to say when she does," she replied, gently pulling Jake's head down against her shoulder and idly running her fingers through his black curls.

"I guess I didn't pray hard enough, Mama," Jake said out loud, trying to maneuver around all the traffic and find a parking space along the riverbank. The sun was beginning to set, and campers were making their way through the smoke from the barbecue grills, eating their hot dogs while drinking beer. The parade was set to begin in fifteen minutes. Jake was supposed to meet friends and family on down the river some, but he wasn't in the mood for company. He pulled his cooler from the back of his truck, shook open a folded chair with one hand, and sank down while opening a beer with the other. He leaned over and sucked the foam that was threatening to spill onto his lap. He pulled his tan baseball cap low over his eyes and leaned his head back while crossing his legs at the ankles. Maybe a few drinks would help clear things up.

Haven meandered through the growing crowd, one eye peeled for Jake, the other for any more familiar faces. She stopped to talk to a few families she recognized from her previous visits, those who loved Harry and those she knew from school. She reluctantly accepted that her perceptions of her hometown were based on the misconceptions of a child. She found it easier this go-around to accept the kindness of folks at face value.

The riverboat parade had started, the first boat being Lucky Louis himself, dressed in purple splendor and throwing plastic beads to the crowd. A boom sounded as a makeshift cannon sent a puff of smoke toward the shore. French music filled with horns and trumpets blasted from the civic center loudspeakers, and drunken revelers hooted in appreciation. The air smelled like charcoal and gas fumes from the Winnebagos stacked together like Matchbox cars in a carrying case. Haven felt out of place, as usual, only this time because she was dressed in tan linen cropped pants with a matching jacket, and her Miu Miu slingbacks weren't doing the job as she made her way down the river.

"Haven? Haven, is that you?" a voice lifted out of the crowd behind her. Roxanne Williams came up to Haven, a tentative smile on her face. She looked the same, beautiful, as always, but Haven noticed her face was fuller, her waist sporting a few extra inches. And the smile on her face seemed genuine, which made Haven instantly suspicious. She took Haven by the arm.

"Hello, Roxanne," Haven said carefully. "How're you?"

"I'm actually pretty great, Haven. Imagine seeing you here. You'd be the last person I would expect to see," she said earnestly. "But I'm so glad I did. You got time to sit with me a minute?"

Roxanne was wearing blue jean shorts with a black tank top and matching cardigan. Her hair was pulled in a haphazard ponytail, and she wore very little makeup. She was barefoot. She pulled on Haven's arm and led her to a pair of lawn chairs set up under a willow tree. Haven had never seen her so disheveled. The soft breeze from the water made the tree look like the arms of a musician gently stroking a harp.

When Haven sat, she turned to Roxanne, anxious to hear whatever put-down Roxanne had in store for her so that she could get on with her day. What she heard was anything but.

Shortly after Haven left Sugar Bend the last time, Mike came off one of his trips in the most ferocious mood yet. Roxanne had not expected him until the next morning, so she had not bothered with fixing dinner. When Mike realized dinner and a beer were not waiting for him upon his return, he lit into Roxanne like she was a piñata at a birthday party.

"I was in the hospital for four days. He broke every rib, my nose, burst blood vessels in my eyes, you name it. They found cocaine and crystal meth in his blood when they tested him at the police station. There was no way I could deny at that time what Mike had done to me. I know you must have heard how he abused me. As much as I was determined to fool the town into thinking we were the perfect couple, it turns out the only fool was me," she said, her eyes clear.

"I did hear, Roxanne. And I'm sorry. But why are you telling me all this now? I don't mean that ugly, but I mean, it's not like we've ever been friends," Haven replied, not unkindly.

"I know. And that's my fault. I guess that's why I'm telling you. The hospital had me visit with their staff psychiatrist before I was released. Those first few visits did more for my state of mind than any antidepressant I ever had. And believe me, I've had quite a few. It made me find the strength to get out, Haven. I know you might not relate because you've always been so strong, but I never knew I had that kind of strength. I sued Mike for divorce, sent him to jail for abuse, and, praise God, his parents made him leave town as soon as his piddly little sentence was served. But I learned during that time that I wasn't ever gonna heal myself until I stopped using other folks' weaknesses to cover my own.

"My therapy took me all the way back to my childhood. I know everyone thinks I lived this charmed life, but believe me, it was anything but. I won't bore you with all the details, but at least my parents were willing to support me in my divorce. They really didn't have a choice once I went public with what everyone knew all along. It really hurts me now to realize how I made a target out of so many people so that I wouldn't be on the receiving end myself. And you were one of my main targets, weren't you? I was so jealous of how collected you were. How you knew just who you were and always went after what you wanted. I couldn't get past that. You struck out of here as soon as you walked off that grass at the football field graduation night. It was obvious you knew right where you were going. I admired that, but I never could let you know." Roxanne didn't tell her about the late nights lying in her bed, listening to her parents argue about which bank teller her daddy was sleeping with that time. She knew her mama wrapped herself up in her diamonds and pearls and social hierarchy as an almost shield to the reality of her world. Roxanne had learned from the best how to put your lipstick on straight and never let the world see you cry.

"But I learned, Haven, that I don't have to live my life in the shadows anymore. My real life, that is. So I guess I just wanted you to know that I'm sorry for all I ever did to you. I hope you'll forgive me," she spoke earnestly, unmindful of the crowd that walked around her, staring only into Haven's eyes.

"Of course I can, Roxanne. I'm beginning to realize we might have all wasted a lot of time building lives around childhood misconceptions. You may be surprised to know that I am the least confident person you could ever meet. When I left Sugar Bend after graduation, I had no idea where I was going. I guess I was running away rather than running to. But I'm here this weekend to right a wrong that should've never been committed. I did it because I was too weak to face the truth. Too scared to accept one of the most precious things ever given to me.

"So I guess we just misunderstood each other. I will forgive you as long as you'll forgive me," she replied, holding out her right hand.

Roxanne took her hand and pulled her to her feet. The two women embraced, allowing the years of resentment and jealousy to melt away in the heat of the Alabama sunset.

"Can you stay and have some dinner with us? I've been dating Scott Davis for about a year now. You remember him? He was a year older than us. Been on the police force for about ten years now. Can you stay?"

"Of course I remember Scott. He always was such a nice guy. But no, thank you. As I said, I've got some unfinished business that just can't wait." Haven turned to take her leave.

"That business wouldn't have anything to do with Jake Baker, would it?"

That stopped her in her tracks. "What makes you say that?" Haven asked, wary of what the gossip mill had produced in the days after she left.

"Well, anybody who had eyes could see the way he felt about you that last weekend you were here. Then after you left, he pretty much went into hiding. We all tried to get him to go out with us, but he never would. Just stayed out there all by himself on the river. The only time I've seen him out was when his mom remarried about six months ago. I don't think he's been on a date since," Roxanne replied, leaning over to get a Diet Coke from the cooler beside the front tire of a blue Jeep Cherokee.

Haven didn't reply, only asked where Roxanne thought she might find Jake. After receiving several possibilities, she gave Roxanne a kiss and thanked her for sharing herself with Haven.

"You stay good to yourself, Roxanne. I wish you and Scott all the best," she replied, letting their hands remain together until only their fingers met as she walked away.

"You, too, Haven. Bye now."

Haven took Roxanne's second suggestion on where to find Jake. Her first one was down by the civic center, where she had seen Brad and Beth setting up a tent earlier in the day. But knowing Jake the way she did and putting that information together with what Roxanne had told her, she figured Jake would rather be alone after their brief run-in that afternoon. She wished she could wait and give him time to cool off. But time was something she no longer had.

CHAPTER 18

S liding her shoes from her feet, Haven walked barefoot toward the landing, careful to avoid broken glass or plastic Dixie Cups that littered the parking lot. Glancing to her right, she noticed a solitary figure under a tall oak, cap pulled down and straight, long legs crossed at the ankles. His arm hung limply over the side of his chair, holding a can by his fingertips. She also noticed about a handful of beer cans scattered at his feet. She made a long loop behind him, allowing her to approach without being noticed.

Or so she thought.

"I thought I made it clear we didn't have anything to say to each other, Haven. Now, I need you to leave me alone," Jake spoke without moving, without even glancing over his shoulder as she made her way to him.

Haven sighed. "I know you did, Jake, and I wish I could respect your wishes. But there are some things to say to you. When you hear what I've got to say, you'll know why you had to listen. Regardless of what you feel about me, I can't leave without your hearing me out," she replied, sitting beside him on the ground after moving around a few beer cans.

"Talk," he muttered, again without moving, his eyes staring directly at the riverboat parade floating in front of them.

"Let me start by saying this, because I have a feeling when I'm done, you probably won't believe me, anyway. But here goes. I made the biggest mistake of my life when I left you. I've never experienced anything like what we shared. Not before and not anytime after. It absolutely overwhelmed me.

"I didn't know what to do with all those feelings. And I didn't think I could survive if I ever lost it. So instead, I chose to give it away. It's one of the many mistakes I've made in my life, probably the biggest. What I've realized over the last few years is that you can't protect yourself from something that's inside of you. And you're inside of me, Jake," she spoke, arms wrapped around her knees. She stopped for a minute, giving herself the courage to continue. Jake still did not move.

"Something wonderful came from our weekend together, Jake. Something I never deserved, but you did. But I took that away from you when I left, especially not even giving you the benefit of an explanation. And for that, I will beg your forgiveness for the rest of my life. It may not make a difference to you now, but there's not been anyone else since you—not that I wouldn't have wanted that. There were times I was so lonely, all I could hear was the sound of my own breathing. Times I had to make decisions that I desperately needed to know were the right ones. But no one could scoot you out of the place in my heart you crawled into that weekend we were together," her voice trailed off, joining Jake in his silence.

Jake reached beside him to take another beer from the Igloo cooler beside the chair, never taking his eyes off the river. He popped the top with one hand and lifted the can to his mouth for one long drink.

"Do you have anything you want to say at this point? Any cussing out, yelling, anything to get off your chest before I really mess things up?" Haven asked earnestly, touching him on the arm.

Jake pulled his arm from hers, her touch scorching his skin through his shirt. Her touch was always like that, almost like the bolts of lightning the summer clouds would throw at each other during a heat storm. He merely glanced briefly in her direction before returning his attention to the nothing he had been staring at previously. He took another swig of beer before he spoke.

"I could have handled your not feeling the same way I did, Haven. I'm a big boy. What ripped my gut was how I could be so wrong with how you felt," he shifted in the chair, staring at her intently. "It took me a long time to get over that, still not sure that I am. But I do know this. I don't trust you, Haven. And it's hard for me to believe anything you're telling me right now. So say what you have to say, and I guess we'll have that good-bye we should have had four years ago."

Haven let the silence hang between them for a few seconds before responding.

"I wish it were that simple, Jake. But it's not," she said, taking a deep breath for strength to continue. "You see, when I said I received something from our weekend together, I meant that. And I meant it when I said I don't deserve it.

"I had a baby, Jake, a little girl. Her name is Lauren Elizabeth Stunham. She's three years old—or three almost four, as she likes to tell people. She doesn't look anything like me. She looks exactly like you. She's amazing and beautiful and a gift from God that I kept from you because I was so afraid you wouldn't want me, and that I would end up losing both of you," Haven was crying openly now, barely able to get the words over the sobs in her throat.

Jake remained silent, the tightening of his jaw the only indication that he even heard what she said. Several minutes passed in silence, the only sounds coming from the crowds and Haven's quiet sobbing.

Finally, Jake spoke, his words as tight as the tension between them.

"Let me make sure I am understanding correctly, Haven. You make incredible love to me. We share things I've never shared with anybody else. You leave without even saying good-bye. And now you come back, almost four years later, to tell me I have a child? How do you even know it's mine?" he asked, his voice getting louder with every sentence. People stared, but he didn't care. He leaned on his elbows, which rested on his knees, running his hands over his face in frustration.

Haven winced at his accusation, but held her anger in check. She knew it was an honest response. She expected no less.

"Lauren's yours, Jake. I named her after your mother. I knew her middle name was Elizabeth, also letting her share Beth's name as well. All you have to do is take one look at her, Jake. She looks just like you. She's got your dark skin, your eyes, your black hair. Everything. And she needs you, Jake, in the greatest way possible," Haven replied, drying her tears with the back of her hand.

Jake was silent for a minute, allowing his mind and his heart to absorb the news.

"What do you mean?" he finally asked.

"She's dying, Jake. She needs a kidney transplant, and I can't help her. She's been sick her whole life with polycystic kidney disease and on dialysis for the past year. But she's rejecting the dialysis and has to have a transplant, or she will die."

Haven spent the next few minutes describing Lauren's condition, why she so desperately needed a transplant. She explained the procedure on how to test for compatibility, what would be required from Jake and his family.

Jake just listened.

"I know I'm asking a lot from you right now, Jake. I can't tell you how many times I picked up the phone even before all this happened to tell you when she first sat up, said her first words, or walked her first steps. But I didn't think that was fair to you. You didn't ask to be a father. It was my decision to keep her. I couldn't burden you with that. I'd already hurt you enough. And I'm sorry to be here now under these circumstances, but you see, I just don't have a choice.

"Please say something. Tell me what you are thinking," she implored.

"I'll tell you what I'm thinking, Haven. I'm thinking just when I thought you couldn't hurt me anymore, you hurt me in the worst possible way," Jake pushed up from the chair, walking around in frustrated circles. "You didn't make that baby alone. Did you honestly think a child would burden me? Do you not know me enough to know we could have figured this out together? Come on, Haven, a baby! I loved you—don't you get that? I fell in love with you the minute I saw you in that funeral home. I probably loved you years before that; I just didn't want to admit it. I gotta have time to think about this. Just give me some time, Haven," he said, walking to the driver's side of his truck and opening the door.

Haven did not want him to leave, especially given the number of beer cans surrounding his chair.

"Let me drive you home, Jake. You've been drinking."

He looked at her hard before replying. "I've only had one beer, Haven. The rest of those beers aren't mine. You see, everything isn't always like you think it is."

Haven backed up from the truck. "Okay, Jake. You win. I'll be at Harry's until tomorrow afternoon. I understand if this is too much too soon. I understand if you tell me to get lost or whatever else you want to say. It's nothing more than I've said to myself a million times or what I deserve. But please don't let your anger toward me cause harm to our daughter," she implored.

"Oh, it's our daughter now? Here's a question for you, Haven: Would you ever have told me about her if she wasn't so sick?" He didn't wait for her answer, simply rolled up his window and drove away. Haven turned slowly, her head bent low as she returned to her car, and left the festivities behind her, unsure of how she would have answered if she could.

CHAPTER 19

It was dark-thirty when Haven returned to Harry's, after stopping at the Pruetts' Quick Stop for some milk, bread, and other essentials to get her through the night. There was no sign of Gracie, only a half-empty food pan and full water bucket by the steps. Haven made a ham sandwich, generously sprinkling salt and pepper over the mayonnaise-laden bread. She ate in silence; the only sounds were the melodious tree frogs singing their lullabies. She glanced down the hall, memories of making love to Jake assaulting her.

After their first coupling on the floor of the den, Jake softly stroked Haven's back. Jake finally nudged her aside and stood up. He easily scooped Haven into his arms and carried her down the hall. As they fell into the bed, Jake took Haven's hair and spread it around her head like a luminous halo. He stretched beside her, leaning on one elbow as he stroked her face.

"What is it?" she had asked him.

"Absolutely nothing. There are no words I would dare say and risk ruining this absolutely perfect moment in my life." He leaned to kiss her, and his hand trailed down her stomach, sending butterfly kisscs on the inside of her being.

Her cell phone rang in her purse beside her, dragging her attention away from the memories she couldn't shake—the memories of Jake and the feel of his hands on her skin.

"Hello," she answered, running a hand through her unkempt hair. She had changed earlier into a velour jogging suit and had built a fire to warm the cool autumn air. She could still hear the distant boom of the cannons as pontoon boats continued to carry on the Lucky Louis parade well after the official one ended.

"Well, sugah, tell me about your day. Anything exciting happen?" Lila's welcomed voice sounded over the line, and Haven yearned to fall into her arms.

"Hey, Lila. How's Lauren?" she asked anxiously, suddenly weary from all the emotions she had battled.

"That little girl is just fine. Don't you worry about her. That sugar-plumb fairy is sitting up like the princess she is in her Aunt Lila's bed watching Friday the 13th part somethin'," Lila replied.

"Lila!" Haven exclaimed.

"I'm kidding, I'm kidding. She's fine, Haven, I promise. I took her by Dr. Jones' office as promised, let his nurse make sure she was okay. And she is, I promise. We're all packed up, ready to hit the road tomorrow. I expect we'll be there late afternoon. Now, quit stalling. Tell me, how'd it go?" Lila knew all about Jake, had spent a good six months trying to convince Haven to tell him about Lauren. She finally gave up, resisting the urge to call him herself when she recognized how much he affected Haven. But for once, she minded her own business and set about trying to fill whatever void she could fill in their lives.

"Not too good, I'm afraid. But about as good as expected," Haven replied, carrying her glass of chardonnay over to the couch before the fire. She lost her breath for a moment, reliving the scene in front of her, watching Jake run his fingers through her hair.

"Is he gonna help? Wha'd he say?"

"Nothing, really. Oh, Lila. I made such a mistake. Whether he would have wanted me or not was not the point. I see that now. The point was we made a child together. And I kept that from him. And now I have the nerve to ask for his help when I wasn't willing to accept his love. How selfish is that?" Haven took a long sip of her wine.

"Not selfish at all, Haven. There's not a selfish bone in your body. You did what you had to do. You're doing what you gotta do. And Jake will have to figure this out for himself. You two need to worry about Lauren right now. Put your feelings aside till that baby is well. Tell him that. It may make any decision he has to make easier if he's not so overwhelmed," Lila said softly, not wanting Lauren to realize she was talking to her mom.

"I would if he would talk to me. I told him everything, Lila. And he just drove away, telling me he needed time. That was about three hours ago, and I haven't heard from him since," Haven replied.

"Well, that's all you can do, Haven. My mama always used to tell me it's never too late for a thank you note and never too late for an apology. If he chooses not to help, well, we'll just cross that bridge when we get there. By the way, I did see that good-looking Dr. Larry today. My goodness, he makes me blush, and that, my dear, is something I just don't do naturally," Lila said.

Haven had not even given Larry a passing thought since she left his house the other day. Strange how just recently, she had entertained the notion of taking their relationship farther, but never followed up on that. Not so strange considering her reaction to Jake today.

"Don't go barking up the wrong tree, Lila. Larry and I are just friends, nothing more. I don't think I can even consider anything else right now. I guess I'll just see you guys tomorrow. Is Lauren where I can talk to her?"

"Sure thing, sugah. Call me anytime tonight if you need to," Lila said, walking back to her bedroom. She shut the door quietly when she realized Lauren had fallen asleep wearing an old tiara that Lila had given her from her pageant days.

"She's asleep, Haven. I didn't realize she'd fallen asleep watching *The Lion King*," Lila whispered.

The two chatted for a few more minutes. "You gonna be okay by yourself?"

"Yes, if anything, it sure does feel good to be home."

"Haven, you are a good person. Nothing in you but good, girl. Don't you doubt that for a second. Jake will see that. You two will figure it out. If he doesn't, then he's not worth the salt on my margarita glass. I love you, honey," Lila said before hanging up.

Lila sat for a minute in the Shaker chair made of knotted pine, circa 1838, in stark contrast to the lime green pillow with fuchsia fringe that Mark had given her for just the purpose of the unexpected. She sighed in frustration.

I put too much faith in that boy, she thought. *I just knew Haven was going home for good. Never did find her home here, try as she did, that sweet thing.* She reached up and turned off the light beside her, closing her eyes for a minute to will her strength to travel across state lines. She realized then that was the first time Haven had referred to Sugar Bend as home.

At the same time, Haven finished her glass of wine, plugged in her cell phone, and pulled her feet underneath her as she lay down on the couch. She fell asleep to her memories of loving Jake in front of another fire so long ago and finding fulfillment in her dreams.

She woke to the sun threading its way across the pine board floors and an incessant knocking on the door. Her watch read way too early as she finger-combed her hair and ran her tongue over her teeth. She opened the door to a rumpled, weary Jake.

"I've got a few things to say to you," he said, pushing past her to make his way into the den. He had not changed since yesterday, didn't appear to have slept, either.

"I'll listen much better after a cup of coffee. Care to join me?" Haven asked, walking to the kitchen without waiting for a reply. She placed two instant coffee bags into mugs she retrieved from the cabinet to the right of the sink and heated them in the microwave. Returning to the den, she handed one to Jake. "Still like yours black, right?"

He took the mug from her without responding. He took a long sip, wincing as the hot liquid raced down his throat. He sank down into Harry's recliner, a defeated look on his face.

"I haven't slept all night. I lay down in the bottom of my boat and just thought about all you said to me. I came here this morning to tell you that I'll do anything I need to do to help that baby out. I would do that whether she was my daughter or some stranger. You know that, Haven. Or at least you should. But the fact remains that I don't know how to trust you," he said, setting the coffee down on the floor and rising to his feet. He hooked his thumbs into his jeans again, shifting his weight to one hip—a stance that would always remind Haven of Jake. He took a deep breath.

"I deserve that and expected that reaction. But it doesn't change the fact that Lauren needs us right now, regardless of whatever road got us here. I know this is selfish of me to ask, and you can trust me when I say that I need to resolve this issue with us as much as you. But can we put that aside until we get Lauren situated? Can we focus on her and worry about us—if there is an us—later?" She employed Lila's advice, unknowing it was the same advice Jake's mama had given him the night before.

Haven had moved to the fireplace, silently drinking her coffee as she leaned against the frame. She was so focused on Jake that she never heard the car drive up, wasn't expecting any company for several more hours. Before Jake could continue, the door flew open, and Lauren ran through, her black hair trailing behind her as she rushed in to find her mother. She was dressed in red seersucker pants and a matching top, her hair pulled to the side in a white bow with red polka dots. She barely glanced at Jake, who had absolutely stopped breathing, before she found her mother.

"Mama!" she exclaimed, throwing herself into Haven's arms. "We got up early! We're here! Is this our house? Who's that?" Her questions were flying faster than Haven could respond. She merely pulled her closer and breathed in the scent of her strawberry-smelling hair. She looked at Jake over their daughter's shoulders and almost sobbed at the wondrous look on his face. He had sunk back down onto the chair, as if his legs just went out from under him. His eyes never left the back of Lauren's head.

"Sorry we're so early," a breathless voice said from the doorway. Lila came in dragging take-out bags from McDonald's and wearing her sunglasses pushed onto her forehead. "THAT baby woke me up at 3 A.M. and would NOT take no for an answer. So we loaded UP and came on and," her voice trailed off as she saw Jake sitting on the edge of the recliner.

Immediately, she dropped the take-out bag on the floor, along with her purse, and walked over to Jake. "My, my, my, Jake. I knew you'd be fine. But honey, I never came close to just how fine you are. Come here, darlin'. Let Aunt Lila tell you the benefits of making love to an older woman."

Leave it to Lila to diffuse a situation, Haven thought. She took a bewildered Jake by the hand and led him outside onto the back deck. He followed her like a patient in the psyche ward being led to breakfast. They stayed outside for at least fifteen minutes. Haven never learned what they talked about. But when they returned, the color returned to Jake's cheeks, and he kneeled before Lauren.

"Hey, Lauren. My name is Jake. I'm so glad to meet you. I'm an old friend of your mom's," he said, holding his hand out to Lauren. He was overwhelmed with the sight of her, his eyes drinking her in like a drop of rain on barren soil. It was like looking in the mirror, although her girliness softened all of his hard edges. She was breathtaking.

"You're not old," Lauren replied, walking past his hand to wrap her arms around his neck. Haven turned her head to hide the tears threatening to spill down her cheeks. Lila did nothing to restrain hers. Jake sat there on his heels, holding his daughter for the first time, rocking back and forth. Over her shoulder, he caught Haven's eyes. "Thank you," he mouthed.

Before Haven could reply, her cell phone rang from where it lay charging on the kitchen counter. She walked quickly over, not wanting to disturb the precious scene unfolding in front of her. Haven recognized Larry's cell phone number on the display and answered the phone hesitantly.

"Hello?"

"Haven, it's Larry. We've got a donor. A young boy was killed in an automobile accident just south of here early this morning, and due to the compatibility, Lauren gets the kidney. It's a perfect match. We've just received the consent of his parents, and we're keeping his organs alive on life support. You've got to get here immediately. This looks good, Haven. I'm very optimistic." Larry was breathless with excitement.

"I'm in Sugar Bend, Larry. It's a good four-hour drive."

"We can't wait that long. I'll call the local hospital and arrange to have a helicopter pick you up. I'm assuming you have a hospital?" Sugar Bend did not, but the county seat fifteen miles away did. After Haven gave Larry the phone number and address of the hospital, he said, "Get there as fast as you can. I'll be here when you land."

Haven got a few more details before she hung up the phone, the least of which was how many could fly in the helicopter. She returned to the den with an ashen look on her face. Conflicting emotions were battling inside her. She wasn't human if she didn't reflect for a moment that one child had to die in order for her child to have a chance at life.

Lauren was teaching Jake a hand-clapping game, and he was clumsily singing "Miss Mary Mack" while Lila was digging out a biscuit from the fast food bag as she sat beside them on the couch. Lila looked over her shoulder and, seeing the look on Haven's face, was the first to speak.

"What is it, sugah?"

"We've got a donor. Larry is sending a helicopter to the hospital to pick us up. They've got to perform the surgery today, or else they lose the organ. We gotta go, but there's only room for one more adult."

Lila didn't hesitate. "Well, you two better get going. I'll meet you there in the few hours it takes me to eat up some Alabama asphalt. I believe my car is still warm. What are you doing staring at me? Take this child to meet her new kidney. Go on, get." Lila rose from the couch, hauling Jake up by the arm and shoving him toward the door.

Haven didn't say a word, didn't have to. The feelings that showed in her eyes toward her dearest friend verbalized everything that was necessary between two people that loved a child.

"Come on, baby," Haven said, picking Lauren up while Jake returned from the back bedroom carrying Haven's bag. "We get to ride in a helicopter to go see Dr. Larry."

Jake had still not said a word, simply opened the door for Haven. He turned and kissed Lila on the cheek.

"Thank you, Lila. You're every bit the friend that Haven described to me four years ago. A true treasure."

"Well, darlin', I know that. I just haven't found a man yet that could afford me," she said with a twinkle and shut the door behind them.

Jake made a few calls from the passenger seat of Haven's car while Lauren bounced excitedly in the back seat. He had spoken at length to his mother last night, telling her the news of Lauren's existence as well as her condition. When Marianne Baker's husband died so unexpectedly, it gave her the perception of people and situations that most normally didn't have. While she was disappointed to have not been told of Lauren's existence, she was grateful to have the opportunity now to spoil a granddaughter. Beth and Brad had DeJesus and were pregnant with another son. While she loved her boys, all of them, the thought of having a girl in her life made her giddy with excitement. But she forced herself to wait patiently until Jake and Haven straightened things out before she got involved. She shared with him as much when she talked to him on the phone late last night.

"We all have choices to make in our lives, Jake honey. Some choices are simple, like what pair of socks is clean enough to wear, or whether to pack a bologna or turkey sandwich in your lunchbox. Other choices make you drink and drive and take a daddy away from a family that loves him. Haven's been alone practically her whole life. She's never really had anyone to teach her about life's choices, try as Harry did. I'm not telling you what to do, baby. I'm just telling you to give it some time before you make your own choices. Just float along for a little while, like you and Brad used to do in your inner tubes.

"You remember how when you waited until just the right time in the early mornings, you could catch the sun peaking around that last bend in the river? Do that now, Jake. Wait till you get to where the river bends to find out what's on the other side. Don't try to guess before you get there."

After getting the call from Jake early the next morning, Marianne quickly threw off the covers and threw on some discarded clothes that were lying in a pile beside her bed. When her husband of six months sleepily asked her where she was going, she merely responded, "To meet my granddaughter."

CHAPTER 20

The flight to Alabaster took less than thirty minutes. It was next to impossible to speak over the noise of the helicopter. Jake kept looking back to check on Haven and Lauren, who was clutching her mother in sheer panic of the ride. Haven was holding her hand while stroking her head with her free hand, her knuckles white and strained. It was impossible to hang onto whatever anger he felt toward Haven when he saw the absolute devotion the two had for each other. His heart flipped a little as his eyes would take in Haven unconsciously, frustrated that she could still have such an effect on him. But he took his mother's advice and pushed those feelings aside. The next couple of days were critical in Lauren's survival, and that was more important than anything.

The helicopter touched down easily on the roof of Memorial. There was only one doctor and nurse waiting to greet them. Jake stepped out of the passenger's side beside the pilot and waited for him to come around to open the door for Lauren and Haven. Lauren leaped into Jake's arms, and he shifted her to one hip as he took Haven by the elbow to help her down. He kept his arm on her elbow as they approached the doctor.

Larry made a quick assessment of the group, noticing the possessive way the man with Haven held onto her and Lauren. Once the helicopter shut down, he offered his hand to the man and said, "I'm Larry Jones, Lauren's nephrologist, and will be assisting in the surgery."

Jake shook his hand firmly as Lauren piped in, "Hey, Dr. Larry!"

"Hey yourself, kiddo," he answered while looking at Haven expectantly.

Haven stepped forward, trying to shake the awkwardness of the situation.

"Larry, this is Jake Baker. He only met Lauren for the first time this morning, just before your phone call. He is a dear friend of mine," she emphasized, widening her eyes and motioning to Lauren. Larry nodded his head in understanding.

"Well, Jake, it is a pleasure to meet you. And let me tell you something. You're going to love getting to know this little creature. Isn't he, Janice?" Larry asked the middle-aged nurse beside him.

"He sure is. Hey, baby doll. We sure have missed you around here. How about you come with Mrs. Janice, and let's go to the little girls' room. We'll catch up with mommy in just a little while," she answered, taking Lauren from Jake as he reluctantly let her go. The two walked off, leaving Larry, Haven, and Jake in an uncomfortable silence.

"Larry, before we get started, there's something you need to know," Haven began. Jake was watching the scene unfold with growing curiosity—from the familiar way Haven used the doctor's name to the hungry way his eyes took her in.

"I only need to know what you want me to know, Haven. I'm not here to judge," Larry replied, folding his arms across his chest. As soon as he looked at Haven with Lauren's father—and there was no denying that's who this was, for they looked identical—Larry knew he was on the wrong side of the coin toss.

"That's just it, Larry. The only person that stands to be judged is me. The truth of the matter is I've known Jake forever. Through my entire childhood, I don't have one memory that doesn't involve him. But when I went back home to bury my father, we found something with each other that I never knew existed. And it scared me to death because it was something I couldn't control if I stayed. So I did what I do best—I ran." Haven paused, looking at Jake to see his reaction. All she found was a blank look on his face while he maintained his customary stance of hooking his thumbs into his belt loops. His hair was disheveled, and the day's growth on his chin gave him a rough appearance. The day was bright and beautiful, in stark contrast to the mood.

"I didn't know at the time that I was taking Lauren with me. And when I found out, I never told Jake. For all the wrong reasons, I kept her to myself. So please don't think this was any of Jake's doings. He knew nothing about Lauren until late yesterday afternoon and only met her for the first time this morning." Haven took a breath, quickly glancing between the two men.

Larry let out the breath he didn't realize he had been holding. That made sense to him. Since he had known Haven, she was always in control, unwilling unless forced to allow someone to help her. "As I said, Haven, I'm not here to judge under any circumstance." He turned his attention to Jake. "But I'm glad to know going forward that you're at least an honorable man. Let's go to my office, and let me explain what's going to happen during the surgery and the next few days," Larry said, walking forward toward the door. Haven followed, her heart hurting with the disappointment she read in Larry's eyes. Jake felt like an intruder as he pulled the door closed behind him.

The rest of the day was a blur. Haven knows she would have dropped into her shoes like the Wicked Witch of the West melted in *The Wizard of Oz* if she didn't have Jake there to support her during that afternoon that seemed to go on forever. While the operation itself would only last some two hours, the entire process would take several more due to pre-surgery prep and recovery. Not surprisingly, Lila breezed in about three hours after leaving Sugar Bend, proving to Haven that she probably didn't even stop to go to the bathroom while driving ninety miles per hour straight to the hospital. But the biggest surprise of the day occurred when the door opened to the waiting room, and in blew Marianne, her new husband, Bill Saltzer, Brad, and his very pregnant wife, Beth. All hugged Haven as if she had included them in her life with Lauren all along. Marianne whispered into her hair, "We forgive you, Haven. The Lord knows you've had your troubles to deal with on your own. He sent us here to help deal with those going forward."

Lila talked Haven into letting her take her home to shower and change clothes. Haven did so in record time, returning to the hospital in sweat pants, flip-flops, and wet hair pulled back into a ponytail. Jake just tsked his tongue at the state of her hair and flipped her ponytail, causing her to smile her first genuine smile at him in four years. Haven surprised Jake's family by bringing Lauren's photo albums stuffed with pictures from the day of her birth until just a few weeks prior. The group laughed at Lauren's head-to-toe immersion in her first birthday cake and teared up at all the photos of Lauren taking her dialysis. Those filled the majority of the book. Jake couldn't help but notice the birth certificate with his name listed as the father. Beth scooted closer to Haven as she described how brave Lauren had been during the last year, and how desperately she prayed that this was the end of the journey.

"Well, let's pray now as a family," Marianne said, rising to her feet. The others joined her, holding hands while Marianne lifted a soft prayer that the God she followed so faithfully would watch over her granddaughter when she needed her most.

"Our most gracious heavenly Father, You tell us in Your Word to give thanks in all things. So we come to You in thanksgiving for the love and mercy that You shower upon us each and every day. We pray, Lord, if there is unconfessed sin among us that You wash us clean so that we may enter into Your presence clean as the driven snow. We pray most of all, Lord, for Your presence in that surgery. Guide the doctors' hands and hold that baby's head in Your lap so that soon we may all show her the love we feel for her. But we know it is nothing compared to the love You feel for her. We pray this in the precious name of our Lord and Savior, Jesus Christ. Amen." The group said a collective "amen," and Haven felt an unfamiliar feeling wash over her—peace. She knew what happened that afternoon was completely out of her control. There was not one thing she could do to produce the outcome she desired. And yet Marianne's words washed over her, taking away the anxieties and unrest she had felt her entire life and filling her up for the first time with peace and security. She breathed in the feeling and held her breath, allowing it to permeate her tissue and reside permanently in her soul.

Haven closed her eyes. *Thank You, Lord, for whatever happens today. I submit to Your will; I submit to Your power. Teach me how to live a life at Your mercy through faith in Your love.* It was her first prayer of salvation and not for selfish motives. Marianne was watching Haven carefully, noting her chin tilted slightly toward heaven. "Give that baby rest, Lord," Marianne lifted up.

No one heard the door open, and Mark entered as he kept his head bowed for a few extra seconds. Mark kept his silence until Haven looked up and saw him.

"Hey, little girl. What's this I hear about a party, and nobody invited Uncle Mark?" he said in a light attempt at humor. Haven folded into his arms and cried tears that she could have sworn were all cried out of her body. He held her in a tight cocoon and swayed gently with her for a few minutes.

As the afternoon dragged on, the group broke into smaller numbers. Mark and Brad were huddled in a corner discussing the multiple delays in the progress of the bridge construction. The Department of Environmental Management had filed several lawsuits to halt construction due to finding an osprey nest near the site. It had taken more than two years to clear the courts and resume construction. Lila, Beth, and Marianne were going at it like long-lost sisters, as Marianne's husband had excused himself to "see a man about a horse."

"Every time I ever go see a man about a horse, I end up married to the man and selling the horse. You'd think I would learn and do just the opposite," Lila had laughed in her customary humor.

Haven was alone in the corner when Jake returned from the vending machine carrying a Diet Coke in each hand. With a sigh, he crossed the room and handed one to her.

"Thanks," she said, popping the top. "You okay?"

"I don't think you need to be worried about me. It's strange, though. I just met that baby this morning, but I feel like my whole world is wrapped up inside those doors over there. I have had trouble breathing the whole afternoon. How is that?" he asked, speaking his words in chopping sentences over the lump in his throat, running his fingers through his rumpled hair as he took the empty chair beside her.

"I know, Jake. I felt the same way the very first time I held her in my arms. It was as if I had known her and loved her my whole life. And just when I think I couldn't love her any more, I just simply do. Jake, let me say something," she began, turning in her chair to face him.

"Don't, Haven. Please don't tell me you are sorry. Looking at those pictures, hearing you talk about all you've experienced by yourself with no one to really help you, you don't owe me an apology. If anything, I owe you one. I came onto you at a time when you were probably the most vulnerable you had ever been. I mean, your father had just died, and here I was trying to get in your pants. And then I don't take any kind of precaution? I mean this isn't high school. My mom always taught me that I had an obligation to respect a woman's body. As much as I loved being with you, I disrespected you that night. And it was wrong, period.

"Listen, Haven, I don't know what's going to happen between the two of us. All my life I've felt the burden of making quick decisions. The older I get, the more I realize that comes from being responsible for my family at such a young age. There was just so much to take care of since we didn't have Daddy. And I love Brad, but we both know he's not always the most responsible. I'm learning that I've not allowed my heavenly Father to help me. And I think it's about time I do before it's too late.

"I will forgive you only if you forgive me. And let's work together from now on, regardless of whatever we decide, on making sure Lauren has the best life possible. We'll do it through prayer, together. And maybe we can figure out how to trust each other along the way," Jake said, gently outlining Haven's jaw with his thumb. Haven allowed the feelings to pour over her. As she looked around the room at those that loved her, she allowed herself to trust that love for the first time in her life. And a strength that came from each one's submission to a higher power made her sit up straighter and dry her tears.

There was Marianne, who had faced one of the most awful circumstances life can throw, but had picked herself up through her faith in God. She found a new life with a new husband without ever losing her Lord. There was Brad and Beth, who found love in the middle of a horrible situation, turning it into a glorious one. And Lila, who worshiped just being alive and showering others with that same enthusiasm. She even thought of Ruth, whose incessant knowledge of things gave her peace in the fact that all things had an answer in her world.

Finally, she glanced at Mark, who just wanted someone to give him permission to be loved by Jesus and to love Him back. It seemed to Haven as if he found that in this room, as he was quietly praying together in the corner with Marianne and Beth. It struck Haven that everyone had to listen to Jesus in the voice He spoke to them, rather than trying to fit their faith through someone else's expectations. Those in the room had found that joy—including her. Her personal Jesus was in this patchwork fabric of a family gathered in this room, united through an unconditional love for a little girl and her mama. She turned her face to Jake and merely nodded.

The phone rang on the volunteer desk beside the door to the waiting room, getting the attention of everyone in the room.

"Miss Stunham, Dr. Jones would like to see you and Mr. Baker in his office, please," the elderly lady said while replacing the phone to the receiver. The two couldn't get to the office fast enough. It seemed forever before Larry joined them.

Both Haven and Jake stood when the door opened, and Larry walked through, taking off his surgical mask. Haven searched his face, but could find no reaction.

"Well, is she okay? Was it successful? What happened?" Haven asked rapidly, firing questions, all the while fearful of the response. Jake took her by the arm and pulled her close to him. She could feel him trembling.

Larry broke into a smile. "I couldn't have asked for it to have gone any better. Dr. Thomaston is the best in the country; I wouldn't have had any less leading the surgery. He told me that she sailed through, although I witnessed it for myself. Now, all we need to do is watch her in recovery and start her on the antirejection medication Prograf. The next few weeks will be critical in knowing whether this will take or not. But it looks like all our prayers have been answered, Haven," Larry responded, taking Haven into his arms.

Jake held his jealousy in check, knowing there was time in the future to satisfy his curiosity about Haven and Dr. Jones. All he cared about at that moment was the fact he was granted the gift of a second chance with his daughter. He couldn't wait to start his life with her.

"Thank you, Dr. Jones. I've learned over the last couple of hours what a role you have played in Lauren's care. I wish I could have been here all along, but I'm sure as hell glad you were," Jake said, shaking Larry's hand enthusiastically.

"It has been my pleasure. These are two remarkable girls, Jake. Don't forget that," he added, almost sternly. Although he had conceded defeat as soon as he saw Haven with Jake, he was unwilling to let go without at least communicating the treasure he was losing. Jake looked him in the eye and acknowledged his words with no response.

"Now, let's talk about the next few days." Larry held out his arm, offering the couple a seat across from his desk while taking a seat on the other side. "We'll monitor Lauren in the recovery room for several hours before we move her to the step-down unit. Then we'll begin administering the antirejection medication and watching for signs of rejection."

"What signs would those be?" Jake asked, his recent arrival on the scene making him an amateur in the battle Haven had been fighting for years.

Haven began speaking, holding a hand up to Dr. Jones. "We'll have to watch her fever carefully. Anything over one hundred degrees is serious. Other things like flu-like symptoms, pain or tenderness in the transplant sight, retaining fluids, things like that could indicate rejection," Haven said, reflecting her knowledge gained from hours pouring over Internet sights and reading medical journals.

Larry nodded. "Don't forget how we taught you to take her blood pressure. You need to watch for a sudden rise or change. You need to pay close attention to the change in color or smell of her urine; also the amount, watch if there's a change there as well. You see, Jake, Lauren's immune system can't tell the difference between a harmful invader and her new kidney. That's why she has to take medication to suppress her immune system to keep this from happening," he said. "We'll keep her in the hospital for about six days and, depending on how well she's doing, she can go home then with the promise of few visitors and lots of washing hands. The next three months are very critical, for if she is going to reject her new kidney, it would be during that time. After that, we're down to a few check-ups a year and a regular life of ballet recitals and T-ball."

"Can we see her?" Jake asked anxiously, already rising from his chair.

Larry nodded back and walked toward the door. "Why don't you two come with me? I'd like nothing better than to have Lauren wake up to your two faces. We'll stop on the way to let the rest of the group in on the good news," Larry said. And the three made their way down the elevator, almost running to their little girl, who was currently dreaming of her mommy's river that she had only heard about in stories.

None of them could have imagined that at that moment, a microscopic germ that had landed in Lauren's catheter during pre-op was marching its way through her system, determined to get all the attention that her body should be giving to her new kidney.

CHAPTER 21

Haven could hear the crowd gathering down the river for the celebration of the new bridge. The old bridge stretched across her boundaries in innocence, unaware that soon she would be nothing more than rubble at the bottom of the river's belly. No one found it unusual that Haven didn't have the heart to go. The last few months had literally strangled any thought of celebrating right out of her and left her with apathetic limbs. After years of organizing every minute around Lauren's health and suddenly not having that, she was listless, unsure what to do with herself. She knew she had so much for which to be grateful. She had learned that God refined you through trials like these, and while she wasn't grateful for them, she remained grateful in them. She was lucky in so many ways. At least she could keep telling herself that. She knew if it wasn't for Lauren's illness, she would not have Jake today. But there were times like this when she reflected too long on Lauren that even her great love for him could not surmount the walls of just plain tiredness that seeped through every pore in her skin. It was these days she just sat on the dock and watched the water.

And those that loved her let her.

She heard the door slam behind her and turned. The sound disturbed her, and she was annoyed. Whoever it was, she just wanted them to go away and let her sulk.

But that wasn't going to happen.

Her smile brightened as she watched her daughter make her way to the dock. She had just celebrated her birthday last week with the kind of party Haven always imagined all the other girls of Sugar Bend enjoyed while growing up. Lauren's Mimi, as she began calling Marianne as soon as she was aware that she was her grandmother, invited every child in Sugar Bend even remotely Lauren's age, regardless of color or sex, to the city park. Ponies and blow-up trampolines entertained the kids for hours. It was four birthdays rolled up into one.

Haven didn't relax the entire day, anxious at Lauren's exposure to so many people. While she forced herself not to hover over Lauren in the nine months since her surgery, she merely panicked from a distance with a pasted smile to the rest of the world.

The infection from the surgery lasted only a few days. It was enough to rock Haven's world and send her to her knees, her newfound faith tested immediately. But Lauren's spirit alone willed that spiteful germ to get lost. She was sick of being sick, and that was it. She knew a little boy had died so she could live. And that was enough for her to demand of her body to get on with it. She had to live, not only for herself, but also for that little boy.

And seeing her daughter enjoy all the attention she never had growing up made up for the tremors Haven experienced in her stomach. And the birthday party went off without a hitch.

"Hey, baby girl. What are you up to?" Haven got up to her feet, holding her arms open to her daughter.

Lauren skipped into them, wearing blue jean capri pants and a white shirt that was loose and flowing. Her feet were bare, and her skin glowed with a healthy tan. It was midsummer, but an early afternoon rain had cooled the temperatures to barely tolerable. It was still the kind of day that pooled in the soft places behind your knees and in the bend of your elbows. The bridge ceremonies went on as planned.

"How come we can't go to the party, Mama?" Lauren asked.

"Well, honey, I guess I just let myself get sad. Sometimes I do that when I think about all you've been through."

"But I'm okay now, Mama. Why're you sad now?"

Out of the mouths of babes.

"Why indeed, baby. Let's do it." As Haven turned toward the house, she noticed Lauren still staring at the river.

"What is it, baby?"

"I love the river. It's just like Jesus."

Haven stood looking at the undisturbed water in front of her, the color of chocolate milk. There could be no water activities due to the bridge ceremonies, so the waters were calm and quiet.

"Like Jesus? How's that?" she asked, curious to know how a four-year-old related the two.

"Because it's always there." Haven was again reminded of a verse she'd recently learned about entering into the Kingdom as little children. Children who don't complicate their love of God with theologies and the world's expectations; they just love.

Haven reached out and held tight to Lauren, grateful that she knew that love at such an early age, but even more grateful that Haven knew it now herself. And so they went, both barefoot with hair in ponytails, to join the roaring crowds along the riverbanks. They made it just before "boomtime" as the flyers advertising the festivities promoted.

Lauren quickly found her family, stretched out on blankets with baskets of chicken and jugs of tea scattered among them. "Hey, Mimi!" Lauren cried out, throwing herself into Marianne's outstretched arms. Haven had to constantly bite back her self-recrimination for stealing the first few years of Lauren's life from her grandmother.

"What about me?" Marianne's husband, Bill, asked in an offended tone as he kneeled beside the two.

Haven turned into Bill's arms. "Well, I love you, Poppa," Haven said enthusiastically, loving the fact that this family accepted her so easily after all she had done.

"I love you more, Poppa," Lauren cried, leaving Marianne's arms to throw her arms around Bill's neck.

Haven looked up at Marianne and smiled. The two exchanged knowing looks, and Marianne simply nodded back to Haven. *Rotten,* they communicated with each other, fully aware of the other's responsibility in spoiling Lauren Elizabeth Stunham.

"Look over there, Haven," Marianne said as she pointed toward the boat landing. Standing with a group of men that included the governor, two state representatives, and the mayor was Haven's husband, Jake. He was wearing his blue jeans, but with a new shirt and boots that Haven had bought him just for this occasion. He looked handsome and impor-tant as he talked politics with the group. It reminded Haven of how her father must have looked all those years ago when he successfully fought the removal of the old mill buildings that now cast their shadows on the partygoers.

The two had married on the dock of Harry's home about a month ago. There was never any doubt to anyone who saw them together that it would happen, and they told Lauren fairly early that Jake was her daddy. It was surprisingly non-eventful, as Lauren assured them, "Course he is."

It just took the two grown-ups a little longer to catch up. They were so wrapped up in Lauren's recovery from her surgery that they fell into a routine as if they'd partnered in the process all along. Jake remained in Sweetgrass, keeping

Lauren while Haven continued to work her remaining listings. Lila would hire Jake on occasion as a handyman on the agency's rental properties as the need arose. The couple had regular dinners with Lila and even Larry, who accepted early on that he no longer had a chance with Haven—that is, if he ever had one.

It wasn't until they passed the three-month mark, that tangible check on the calendar that signaled the "all clear as it can be" to transplant recipients, that they began to act on the feelings they kept dormant for so long. Jake, however, refused to make love to Haven again, vowing to not touch her intimately until he could touch her as his wife. They remained in separate bedrooms, Lauren alternating which bed she ended up in the middle of the night. But their love and unrequited passion grew to an intensity that could only culminate into the all-important question Jake posed to Haven one night after putting Lauren to bed.

Haven was finishing up the dishes, while Jake made himself comfortable on the couch. It had taken some time for him to feel at home in Haven's house because it was so proper. Everything matched with stylish flair, from the nail-trimmed leather sofa to the recliner that seemed as if no one had sat in until him. Haven admitted to him after a couple of months that she wasn't sure if she even felt at home there yet or not, but it seemed to fit that time in her life.

Haven returned to the den, carrying a glass of sweet tea in each hand. Jake took his, but placed it on the glass coffee table and pulled Haven down beside him. He stared at her intently before speaking.

"What are you doing?" she asked, a little nervous. She put her glass beside his on the table. She had felt something different stirring in Jake lately. He had long periods of silence followed by solitary walks on the beach that led Haven to believe he was trying to figure out a way to leave her. That familiar feeling of panic stirred in her gut.

"I'm looking at your ribs," he said, sliding his hands over her T-shirt.

"Excuse me?"

"Your ribs. You see, Mama used to tell me that when God created woman, he took a rib from man and used it to form her. She said I would always recognize my wife by looking for my rib. In other words, she said you had to recognize the inside of a woman in order to know if she's right for you."

Haven sat perfectly still while Jake rubbed his hands up and down her rib cage. She didn't realize she was holding her breath. Suddenly, he stopped, but kept his hand on the last one.

"Yep. That's it. I thought I recognized it."

"What are you saying, Jake?"

Jake took his hands from Haven and reached into the pocket of his jeans. He bent down on one knee, taking Haven's left hand into both of his, and placed a small, marquise diamond on her left ring finger.

"I'm saying that I'm ready to get my rib back. It's been awfully uncomfortable without it. I'm saying I'm ready for us to be a family. I'm saying I'm ready for you to be my wife. But I gotta know if you can come back with me to Sugar Bend. Because I think Lauren needs to grow up around her family. Can we do that, Haven? Can we go home to be a family?" Jake knew that was the harder question. He had no doubt that Haven loved him. What he wasn't sure about was whether she could receive that love from him and leave all that she had forged for herself in Sweetgrass to return to Sugar Bend.

Haven surprised him.

"Yes, Jake. Yes, I'll marry you. Yes, we can be a family. And yes, we can live in Sugar Bend, as long as we live on the river. Honestly, I can't think of anywhere else I'd like to raise Lauren. And I just can't seem to recall any reason I left to begin with."

And so in a moonlight ceremony on the riverbank in Sugar Bend as Lauren stood between her parents, the three recited their vows together. The sound of the river water gently flowing behind them provided the background music. They moved into Harry's house, with Jake promising to renovate, adding an extra room for Aunt Lila to visit. Haven put her real estate career on hold indefinitely, which was fine with her. She had found all she never knew she was missing, but yet all she could ever want that afternoon in the hospital room. She had learned on that day also to trust the love she so wanted to give away. It was time now to make it official.

Suddenly, a hush fell over the crowd as the mayor stepped up to the microphone.

"Ladies and gentlemen, may I have your attention, please," the portly man said, clearing his throat. "We are gathered today on the shores of our great river to say good-bye to the bridge that once played a vital role in the growth of our city. But time, as it does with most of us, took its toll on that old bridge," he said, grabbing his girth and eliciting a chuckle from the crowd, "so, thanks to our great governor, who is in attendance today, along with our state representatives, we are able to say good-bye and let her rest in peace.

"As you all know, we held an essay contest to see who would press the detonation button. And I couldn't be more proud to introduce the winner to you, whose poem 'Second Chances' just blew us away. No pun intended. Jake Baker, will you come on up here?"

The crowd rose to its feet as Jake took the microphone. He waved his hands to quiet them down and began to speak. "Most all of you know me well enough to know how uncomfortable I am with all this. But I have to admit, I cheated a little bit in this contest," he said as the crowd hushed.

"My daughter, Lauren, helped me write this poem. You see, we could have lost her nine months ago, but we were given a second chance. So it's really with her inspiration that I wrote this poem. But I also dedicate it to my daddy, who would have given anything for that bridge to have given him a second chance. Well, here goes," he said, clearing his throat before his emotions got the better of him, retrieving a piece of paper from his back pocket and unfolding it.

Haven glanced at Marianne, whose eyes shone brightly through her tears. Lauren bounced between her mama's lap and her Aunt Beth's, who had joined them with Brad, DeJesus, and their infant son, Trey. Finally, she met her husband's eyes across the crowd, and everyone around them just "poof" went away. Although he held the paper in front of him, he spoke from memory, never losing eye contact with Haven.

> *The river gives us second chances*
> *Third, fourth, and fifth ones as we need.*
> *Each visit cleansing us of broken dances;*
> *As the Lord takes our tears to the sea.*
> *Treasure the times that we fall short*
> *Wrap them up in memories.*
> *But like the river, dwell no more*
> *On life's ill-gotten revelries.*

The crowd roared its appreciation, coming to its feet once again as Jake made his way to the detonation machine. The state had hired an engineering firm out of Atlanta to ensure the dynamite was strategically placed so that the bridge would crumple into tiny pieces, easily absorbed by the river. Jake stopped in mid-stride, turned, and walked back to the microphone.

"I would like for my wife and daughter to join me," he said, motioning to Haven, who took an exuberant Lauren's hand and made her way to her husband. The two stood beside Jake as he prepared to push the button, while the crowd fell immediately silent in anticipation. Haven stepped back, closed her eyes, and waited, returning to a dream that she had not visited in quite some time—only this time, she realized that while the bridge was destroyed in her dream, reality would provide a new bridge over which to cross.

Suddenly, the boom sounded, and the bridge collapsed as planned. Haven looked at the bend in the river as it shook from the detonation and pushed the water back toward home. *Our home*, she reminded herself, and took her husband's hand after he lifted Lauren to his shoulders. They said good-bye to friends and family, waving off invitations to dinner. Jake left his truck at the landing and took the keys from Haven as he opened the door for his family. Glancing at the floorboard, he noticed a shoebox.

"What's that?" he asked as Haven held the seat up for Lauren to climb into the back.

"You know, it's funny. I found this shoebox when I was here going through Harry's things the weekend he died. I forgot to go through it, so I put it in the car to remind me. I just keep forgetting to take it out. I'm sure it's nothing but old pictures, report cards, or something. We'll take a look when we get home," she replied.

Jake returned to his side of the convertible and lowered the hood. The family joined the long line awaiting entrance to the new bridge as the governor cut the ribbon. As they waited, Jake looked over at his beautiful wife sitting beside him and the precious gift he could see in his rearview mirror. He then looked across his wife and was grateful for the life that waited for him where the river bends.

Printed in the United States
94990LV00003B/130-999/A

9 781604 772715